Also by Brad Land

Goat

PILGRIMS

UPON

THE

EARTH

PILGRIMS

UPON

THE

EARTH

A Novel

Brad Land

Random House

New York

Copyright © 2007 by Brad Land

Published in the United States by Random House,
an imprint of The Random House Publishing Group,
a division of Random House, Inc., New York.

RANDOM HOUSE and colophon are registered trademarks
of Random House, Inc.

Grateful acknowledgment is made to Wesleyan University Press
for permission to reprint "Pilgrims" from *Door in the Mountain:
New and Collected Poems, 1965–2003* (Wesleyan University Press) by
Jean Valentine, copyright © 2004 by Jean Valentine. Reprinted by
permission of Wesleyan University Press.

ISBN 978-1-4000-6380-2

Printed in the United States of America on acid-free paper

www.atrandom.com

2 4 6 8 9 7 5 3 1

First Edition

Book design by JoAnne Metsch

for George Elmer Howell and Rebecca Howell

for Sarah Strickley

Standing there they began to grow skins
dappled as trees, alone in the flare
of their own selves: the fire
died down in the open ground

and they made a place for themselves.
It wasn't much good,
they'd fall, and freeze,

some of them said
Well, it was all they could,

some said it was beautiful, some days,
the way the little ones took to the water,
and some lay smoking, smoking,

and some burned up for good,
and some waited,
lasting, staring
over each other's merciful shoulders,
listening:
            only high in a sudden January thaw
or safe a second in some unsmiling eyes
they'd known always

whispering
Why are we in this life.

JEAN VALENTINE, *"Pilgrims"*

There was nothing on the beach, only the waves, the hard sand,
and the spray. The beauty I sat on ran to the verge of his
heartburst. I had never given the horse a name. I suppose I was
waiting for him to say what he wanted, to talk.
      But Christ is his name, this muscle and heart striding under me.

BARRY HANNAH, *"Dragged Fighting from His Tomb"*

PILGRIMS

UPON

THE

EARTH

1

THE NORTHWEST corner of the state was mostly hardwood and granite, and the cold water from the rocks moved fast and splintered east, and in the trees beside the swift water, mills broke cotton to cloth and bent steel red into girder and joist and brace. Near the town rocks bore up gray in the woods, and some had water run over them, and spots worn smooth, and moss in patches, loud green, and some had old Indian words scratched at their faces. In spring, bears stirred the woods and sunned on the rocks.

Late June and fourteen he wandered among them and put his small rough hands for a long time against the old letters carved on the rocks, and they were more like pictures, birds and wolves and people mixed together, and he twisted the ends of his fingers raw in the grained divots, and went farther this time, kept when his boots sank ankle deep in the old leaf blown drifts in the birch and the laurel and the sapgum.

From the thick growth he came to an outcrop; for a moment the full light pinched his eyes; he looked through cotton, dime spots fuzzed pink flowerheads at his eyelids. He blinked hard on the rock face; naked, wide, a slow grade. The light then sharp and clear edged, the bear focused twenty feet past. It was small, and sat hind legs like a person, black hair stuck to wet licks, face tilted at what seemed a pondering of the light. He saw end days, a monster in the woods. He held, lock still, swallowed low breath, waited for the bear to get his smell then gallop; open mouth, white teeth.

He remembered two; a bear on the television toppled trashcans and stood up and batted the air and mad spit in its bawl and charged a man back turned and running. The other one, in the museum downtown, rifle shot at the kidney and head when it lost the woods, lumbered at the sidewalk near the jewelry store and gutted a couple leaving through the glass door; four small bells, like ones collared to a sheep's neck, were tied at the push handle with a red bow from winter holiday; they rang when the door flapped; the county packed the bear once dead with cotton and wood shaving, wheeled it to a spot in the center of the dusty collections room below the frayed white war flag with the rattlesnake coiled on its face, and fixed it in a high standing pose, one arm raised chin level, a warning swipe, jaw stretched a yell, claws glued black keys. His grandfather's spotted right hand was gripped to the red felt theater rope that squared it off, his index finger, thumb to the first knuckle, shot off in the second big war. A heavy brushed silver band took up most of the stub; he tapped the ring against a joint on the brass pole, pondered up at the stuffed bear for a long time, didn't speak, squeezed his tack-hard fingers on the rope and then let go.

The bear on the rock turned its head, the rest of it kept still, and calm. He stayed fixed to its eyes, leather brown muzzle dipped like a push swing, and held the first step, the run he felt winding bed springs at his forefeet; the small water in the woods behind him gurgled; the trees clapped. The bear stood to all fours and huffed, shifted front weight from one shoulder flank to the other and swiped at the rock. His left boot twitched; the bear lumbered ten feet his way and stopped quick, backed a foot and swatted the air this time, like an underhand pitch, a chin jab. The fingers on his right hand tapped his belt at the hip; he wished to pull a gun. The bear panted, stayed looking at him. Then it sat down to its rear again, fell its head back to the light stretched warm over the rock face. A cloudrack grew dark rain in the south. His outer thighs clenched, fine hair stood on his forearms; he felt weather changing.

Branches slapped his forearms held face level and bare, and some split and broke off, and he ran fast in the woods, legs and feet scaled fell trees; horses might feel like this, dogs maybe, heart in the eyes, busted from a screaming hand.

His father, the foreman, the widower, the tired man, forty-two years his senior, told him black bears ran forty miles an hour, flat out, and he thought of this. But the bear he left on the rock, drunk on light and warm half sleep, would not come after; still, it felt like a pardon, and he didn't stop until the trees walled, turned a row tilled corner field, moss gray and wet, rain three days past still there, but drying quickly, didn't stop until he saw the back of the house, red shutters at the windows, and that was far enough.

2

AUGUST ELEVENTH he turned fifteen and legal to drive with an adult, and then two days after that Terry Webber started at the high school. He was named for a champion racehorse from northern Virginia called Terrence's Cotton Mather, and for his father, the second shift foreman at Hardwick Textile in Issaqueena, South Carolina. Sometimes he lingered in the woods at mounds for dead Cherokee and looked for parts of them still there. His chin and cheekbones were severe, angry in a way he did not mean, and his neck down onto his chest was splotched red, cold outside or not. The front tooth on his left hand side was dark gray from a yellow plastic bat he took to the mouth in second grade. He was narrow in the legs and shoulders, didn't figure himself any kind of strong, but the easy way he broke some things surprised him, a fury, a dogfight there he didn't consider.

His father, Benjamin Webber, turned fifty-seven on the eighteenth day of that month, and at work, brown sweatshirt, short on his knobbed wrists, plastic goggles, corded tight at the back of his head, he waited for the last one running the dye vats to punch out, squared the front latch in the truck bay, shut the lights in the break room and unplugged the soda machine from the wall socket, took a cardboard box of twenty brick red sweatshirts stitched that day, and put them to his trunk. The next afternoon he traded them, plus two hundred dollars, to a man called Nola Walker for a gunmetal blue hatchback. He was well known, Nola Walker; besides two square miles of junked cars he owned a firework warehouse, a service station, a petting zoo with a Bengal tiger and a howler monkey that ate cigarette filters, a mile racetrack for dirt bikes.

Benjamin Webber left the keys on the small table in the kitchen, two of them, attached at a paper clip; Terry kept to paved roads the first week, learned the feel of the brakes, to press them long before he wanted to stop, the northwest drift of the wheels, places where the engine held, and where it ran full on. He learned often, when rolled down, the passenger side window got stuck, and that the navy ceiling cloth drooped from the metal, ballooned close to his scalp like a pup tent, blown wind taut. Then he wanted the dirt roads and went ten minutes on a wet side path close to the school. He ran a long puddle too fast, and the back end sank, tires necked rim high in the bog, and then the car was stuck, and required chain.

He didn't put it on right. When the tow lurched the chain noose slid to the driver's side and pulled the fender out close to a foot at the corner. He left it that way, and the car got wet in the rain, the lip rusted sharp and bowed. Twice he bumped a leg against it in the school lot, and cursed, leapt to the other foot and held his shin with two hands.

It took an afternoon for him to color the wide rust spot on the hood with a blue permanent marker he lifted from the mercantile; he'd taken, as well, a metal ring for his keys. He hovered at it like homework, a science experiment.

3

SEPTEMBER HE saw Alice Washington, a junior twice held back, seventeen and eight months, huddled in the smoking section behind the science building first, and a few days after he stood close to the hall glass across from the library and saw her through the top pane in the second marked cigarette yard, leaned against the west brick wall, close to the high fence. She bit a white filter between her teeth, wore an ash gray hooded sweatshirt, NORTH PLATTE in red box letters on the chest. She looked like he thought mountains must when sunlit. On his left the ones old enough or with an adult signed letter rocked the double glass doors and went on their smoke outside, the space square, like a dog pen, green painted concrete, heel cut, chain link, walled in by math building and woodshop. Past the fence, the parking lot rashed in the early, high yellow light, and even farther, the lodgepole treeline swayed.

She turned at the hips and clamped her hands in the gaps shaped like road signs and shook the wire. A few more pushed through from inside. She let go the fence and turned back. Her hair was long, brass colored, pinned high on the sides, spot on her neck shaped the mouth of a teacup, more olive than the rest of her. Terry touched dents on his forehead worn by chicken pox, a cluster above his left eyebrow the pattern of birdshot. He let his hair back over, in his eyes. It smelled of batteries, old smoke. He got a long piece to his mouth and chewed. It tasted of rope, tilled dirt.

He turned to the library glass behind him and put a hand over his eyes at the glare. A student helper pushed a metal shelving cart, another wiped at an overhead projector, tin cases and bookspine high walls around them, and the librarian, a man shaped like a greyhound, swayback and narrow, pulled drawers from the card cabinet at the middle of the long room and ran his fingers across the letter tabs. A screen map on the back wall of the library, big as a rain tarp, laid bare the lines of the Soviet Union.

Terry remembered television, the actor president and his shined rock black hair standing at a podium, talking to whoever was watching, speaking on the urgent need for machines with lasers in outer space; it worked like a big net, a web, he said, and evaporated nuclear missiles shot from Russia into space dust. Terry didn't understand, not any of it; not lasers, or space webs, bright red mushroom clouds or soldiers in the snow with machine guns and dead kingfishers on their heads. He'd turned the switch on the kitchen black and white and set back some of the foil wrapped on the base of the rabbit ears then sat to one end of the kitchen table. What he thought, in the quiet of the box gone, was dammit, and he shook his head and ran his fingers into his matted hair, and they stuck at a knot on top and tangled on both sides, and then he thought some more, and after some time what it seemed was that slick fucker wasn't like anyone he knew, or ever would, and him telling people to be scared of Russians didn't mean anything. The closest was some of the teachers at school, and he knew, for a fact, they mostly said things to keep them scared and in their desks.

Terry moved to the trophy case in the hall and read the names of school champions cut onto plaques. Then he stooped over the bone cabinet and he crouched in front and put his hands on the display glass; jawbone, potsherd, seven arrowheads; he thought of shark's teeth; all of it was sifted from the orange clay nearby. Someone had written, in black ink, on the green mint wall to the right of the display, here is what's left of them. He heard boot soles loud in the hall, and turned around.

Basil Frick galloped, high kneed, hair red sheened, elbowed the double doors, staggered outside and went in a hard leap on the fence. His boots slipped at the toeholds. He got his hands on the top bar, but his weight bobbed him down and his right sleeve caught. He pulled at it with one hand and worked a tear.

Alice Washington kept the cigarette in her mouth and pressed her hands at his calves and pushed up, and Basil Frick dropped on the other side, stumbled, line sprinted to the woods; dust, shell white, spat from his heels. Killdeer weeping in the soy field scattered a wake behind him.

The librarian rushed the hall and threw the doors outside. He ran the concrete and stopped hard on the fence and put his hands at it and shook. He yelled wide mouthed, watched Basil Frick make it to the far trees, turned quick to Alice and stood at her and leered. He wagged a finger. Alice Washington put her head down and pulled a drag. He yanked the cigarette from her mouth and broke it at the middle. She lit another, and he took that one, and stomped it. Next one she blew smoke in his face. The librarian coughed and wiped his eyes and then he gripped her severe on the arm and jerked her to the doors.

Watching this welled a burn in Terry's throat; he wished to say it, but could not: let go of her arm, son of a bitch, it hurts, bad, let go.

Alice Washington kept the cigarette past the glass and dropped it inside on the gray carpet. It stayed lit, and kids walked around the low plume. Terry picked it up. He went outside, and slumped down, knees close to his chest, against the east wall, light bleeding over the top of the math wing. One of the special kids they kept playing kick ball in the gym sat a few feet off, put his legs straight out, toes up, spine a drastic hunch. Terry smoked fast. The special kid did, too, and smiled at the fence and the woods between pulls, teeth bleach white, gums worn black and red, the high curve on his right ear chewed off, or maybe bit.

4

BASIL FRICK sat a desk up in the history class, had a red mustache going on two years, and perfect pitch. Once, the history class went on field trip to the armory; when they left the short yellow bus and filed toward the doors the teacher noted the display of eight rusted cannons on wheels from the states' war running the perimeter of the big front yard, Basil drove up on his red motorcycle, stopped where all of them could see. The engine sputtered on the dirt bike; he coughed it, twice, and stared the class down. He pointed at them, then sped off. Afterward, in the yellow bus on the way back to the school, John Michael Johnson said he was sure Basil had a gun, and had just decided, right then, changed his mind, really, not to shoot all of them.

Basil wore a green jacket, army standard, sergeant bars at one arm. An ironed patch at the other sleeve read WAR PIGS, and the chest pocket he crossed the name and wrote BASIL above in black marker. He wrote FUCK PEACE in the same black and small letters at his shoulder. A white scar on the back of his head stood his red hair out to a lick, a map line. He scratched the bare skin and pushed some hair over. His wristwatch was black, a calculator face. He wore work boots, like Terry, dark brown and scuffed bare at the heels and toes. Terry watched the back of his head for a long time with the teacher's voice in his ears a factory hum. He wanted to ask Basil what he ran from, wanted to ask him what he saw past the woods, and if, at the armory, he'd meant to do all of them.

The history teacher, back turned, wrote in white chalk on the blackboard. Basil put his hands on the desk and pushed up on them. He stood, finger pinched a plastic bag at the top seam so it looked as a flag when wind limp. He flapped it around. The bag was filled a quarter way. He wagged it at the kids in their desks, shook the dope around inside, and then he leaned his head back and laid it over his face like a washrag, kept still and balanced, put his hands out at the sides, faked a wobble. Some of the kids laughed with hands to their mouths. Some turned away from him, to the east window, some down to desktops. The teacher turned. Basil dropped his head and let the bag slide off; he caught it with his left hand and put it to a big side pocket, graceful as a pulled gun, a card cheat. He sat down, crossed his fingers and put his hands on the wood.

5

LIGHT RAIN in the night, then morning cold.

The gas tank was empty. He stepped out, kicked at loose rock in the driveway, stood and looked at the car, tossed the key ring over the cracked window to the driver's seat. For a moment he thought of punching the glass
or the door panel, and it took all of him to steady his hands already
curled to fists and trembling. He rapped knuckles against the back end, at
the flap covering the fuel spout, put hands then to his hips and paced.
School was five miles.

He walked in the tall broom grass at one highway shoulder, wet at his shins,
gone dead some at the tips. Yellow headlamps broke the hill a quarter mile
in front, then dropped, sped the incline and turned road wet gone past him,
damped his forehead with rain and brake dust. Other cars hissed at his left
shoulder, early blue light smoked on the hoods. He was tired, eyes strung
sleep. He drifted a foot in the road. Fast air kicked hard at his shoulders,
brimming like an industrial fan, and fell him backward. A red and white
box pickup keeled to the other lane and the old man driving blew the horn.

The high grass bobbed above him. He stayed on his back and kept his legs
long in the damp, crossed them at the calves, and after what felt a long
while but was not things righted in his head, and he thought to stay some
more, but he stood instead and brushed his shoulders and arms, wet spots
at the elbows like patches on a dress coat one of the teachers wore.

Three miles before the front gate the school traffic was quiet and the road bare and dry. He saw a dented spot in the shoulder grass and stopped and leaned over.

He worked one hand beneath the bird, and then he raised it up and cupped it with both. Splinter grass clung to its back and chest, and it was small, warm, brown and white mottled, a finch, a sparrow, he couldn't tell. It didn't look dead; eyes open and wet black, but its head doll limp, small yellow feet gripped an old branch. Maybe, he thought, it was just sleeping; it could wake later and need water, seed before flying. He unzipped his knapsack, moved a notebook over some, put the bird careful on the bottom, and then he sealed the bag and draped it to his right shoulder.

At lunch a teacher paced rows in the cafeteria, checked to see they ate paper carton milk, meat, block green jelly, and left soon as they finished. Most of the hour they spent in the yard. The school was built in a hollow circle, around a courtyard. At the west end there was an amphitheater, maroon painted steps in cracked jagged lines, grass and daffodil and rank clover pushed through. Three basketball goals lipped the east end, near the gymnasium, chain net rusted beneath the high red rims.

Terry hunched with the rest of them on the fence near the amphitheater and kept the bag closed and propped at his shins. John Michael Johnson stood beside him. He was fourteen until November, neared six feet, wore eyeglasses handed down from his older brother that made him look a scientist, the lenses square, thick as bottle glass, arm on the left temple fastened by white suture tape. He tore up his first razor before he turned twelve. He grew block sideburns to his jaw. Terry leaned over the knapsack again and checked the zipper. Then he stood up. John Michael kept the newspaper wide and looked over at him and then down at the bag.

You got something in there? he said.

Nope.

Come on.

Alice Washington and some others on trash detail paced the far end of the steps and carried plastic bags. They bent for soda cans, scrap paper. The principal walked a line above them. Terry shook his head slow.

I don't have anything, he said.

Fine, John Michael said. You just walk up here, like you've got a damn pimp cane and a top hat.

What?

Nothing. You just go on then. There's current events I need to know about. I think some old coot saw that lizard thing.

What?

The monster that lives in the swamp. Half man, half lizard. Or most lizard and a little man. I can't remember.

Like the swamp thing?

No, not like that. It's much worse.

Iguana?

That's stupid.

John Michael went back to the paper and held it up. He was at the front page. He stayed on a picture of Basil Frick, and then he read funeral plans and the names of relatives aloud to a few of them, and then he went on and told the whole thing. Terry thought of a painting, a man clamped wrists and neck at a wooden stock, over him the town crier wearing a curly wig with powder in it, tall red socks, a long red coat and a pirate hat. He'd seen it the year before in the history book. It was from when the British were coming and before they shot the fireworks.

The afternoon prior Basil sat back straight at a tree in his front yard, held the butt of a single-shot twenty-two with his knees and opened his mouth. The bullet bounced around some inside his head, and it didn't come out. His father watched television in the back bedroom. He bled for two hours, from nose and eyes and ears, and then he died.

John Michael held the picture up where they could see; Basil Frick in a suit, hair slicked, mouth turned on a grin.

One of them said, He looks like the damn devil.

Another went, Hello, mister lucifer.

Terry got a cigarette and watched the trash squad some more. Alice Washington worked nearby. He saw her help Basil jump the fence, but he wanted to ask her what misstep put her there on detention, anyway. He thought to use the word vagrancy in his question. He snapped the filter close to her ankles when he finished. Alice Washington kept at the plastic bag and the ground. He kicked a soda can. It scraped at the asphalt, bounced, and she watched it spin and then rest. She turned up, eyes wet gray. Terry waved. She put a hand up quick and dropped it back. She stooped at the can, foot dented, put it to the bag, bent down to another.

John Michael folded the paper and held it pressed between arm and ribs. He spoke loud and waved his hands.

That jackass told me I couldn't sing in music class. I was in the choir. I sang in church. Old ladies got faint. What's he singing? Nothing. That's what I thought.

It's a dumb story is what it is, one kid said.

He was named Richard Jenkins. They caught him jerking it at the town pool the summer before. He had a buzz cut, a large mole on his earlobe shaped like the state of Georgia.

John Michael turned at him quick, tilted his face and closed one eye when he spoke.

What? he said.

I said it's dumb and you heard me say it, Richard Jenkins said.

John Michael raised his voice and stuck his finger out.

You just go on before I fix you up.

He swung his free arm to one side, pointed across the yard at some kids huddled far off.

I said go on.

Richard Jenkins stayed, crossed his arms at his chest, and flared his nostrils wide. John Michael shook his head slow.

That's twice I told you go on, he said.

Richard Jenkins kept his eyes straight and did not turn, even then.

You won't be helped will you? John Michael said.

He held the newspaper to Terry.

Take this, he said.

Terry folded the bundle under his arm the same as John Michael, like a headlock. John Michael spit to one side and took off his glasses, folded the arms and set them at his chest pocket; without them, his face looked a barbell; he stepped close to Richard Jenkins, chin level to his forehead. The yard was quiet, air heavy, like before thunder.

A T THE house he got two sheets of newspaper from the bin and wrapped the bird and laid it back into the knapsack. He pulled the zipper, patted the lump through the canvas. He tried to think of a name but couldn't; something, maybe, about how fast birds fly, how blue their wings, how red their throats. The rooms were empty and still. Most days his father's job held him past dark. The two of them lived in a small wood frame near the baseball field and close to the brown and yellow painted water tower shaped a thimble. There was a red brick fireplace at the fore room, and a short couch and a chair, and a small kitchen with an electric stove, linoleum and tack board cabinets, a window above the sink. The drive was a tire worn dirt circle out front. The neighbor planted three rows of firs in the east side lot to sell at Christmas.

Before the firs, the lot was scrub and dwarf pine, trunks blacked soot, and charcoal. Terry put his hands against them, stained his fingers ash; sometimes then he drew swipes around his eyes and at his forehead. He looked himself in the mirror, made faces, angry and monstrous as he could figure, and sometimes too he made a low growl like he thought a wolf did. The art teacher liked the homework drawings he made with hunks from the trees turned charcoal; house, dog, horse. He thought of his father standing at the kitchen window near first light and look- ing out, fingers gripped hard over the sink lip, face night black, then lit yellow from a small car burned cinder in the tree lot. The ones inside were from the high school, older than Terry by seven years, two boys, the paper said later, dead already, by shotgun, before the car melted, because they messed too long with some dealers from another county and got sticky hands.

Beside the big window in the last house his father rented he saw a dead redbird turned upside down, feet stuck long and old yellow. There wasn't furniture yet. His father pushed the door and led him to the living room, the knee high windowsill, four pane glass taller than his father. They stood there looking out to the yard. Next to his foot some light came through hard and heated the carpet and at first he thought to go and lie down in it but then he saw the bird there and the dust come up around it in the light beam. He pointed it, his father bent down and gathered it up, held it in one hand, but lightly, careful, like he held thin paper. He got the shovel from the washroom, and he told Terry maybe it was bad luck, a dead bird in the house, but he was not sure. Terry asked him how it got there, how it died, and he said he didn't know. Probably it came through the chimney or a cracked door, made for the window, thinking it not a window, but the sky, broke its neck sudden and in such a way to drop it mid thought, there on the green velvet carpet. Outside, Terry smoothed the dirt over the bird once his father dug the hole and placed it there, and let the shovel drop handle long in the yard. His father said maybe they should say a prayer or something.

You know any? he said.

Just one for food, Terry said.

The ring finger on John Michael's left hand was jammed straight to the top knuckle. He curled the other ones down and winced. They sat on his front stoop and watched some cars pass on the street.

That hurt? Terry said.

I'm just making a face. I hit him wrong is all. Cheekbones break hands is what. I was going for his nose.

You dropped him.

John Michael turned a red plastic butane lighter upside down and tilted it to heat the metal. He had three fresh burns at his forearm, down near the wrist.

Turn it all the way that lighter blows up, John Michael said.

He knew this caution from his brother, fifteen years elder, a seller of vacuums that used water to get at the dirt.

The fumes don't have anywhere to go.

He tilted the flame close.

Pow.

He let it down and put the lighter on the step.

I'm telling you it's gone hurt, John Michael said.

I can stand it, Terry said.

He wasn't sure if he could or not, but he wanted to see. Terry put the lighter on his forearm and held it.

I wonder if Basil had a dog, John Michael said.

Terry kept the lighter pressed down, mashed his teeth and pinched his eyes hard at the burn. His open hand shook.

He probably had a fucking cat, John Michael said. Probably bunches of them.

Terry opened his mouth wide and yelled, felt an animal, threw the lighter down against the steps.

Pissing all over things and rubbing their asses on your car. If one ever does, dammit, put an orange on the hood. It doesn't matter where. A cat's scared of an orange. Waiting until nobody's around to see, fucking knocking over vases and shit. A one eared tabby named John Stone hit this Hawaiian statue thing my mom has on the mantel, broke it on the goddamn floor. And I got blamed. Me? That fucking cat. I hope he goes off in the woods and can't fend himself. He'll see then. I ever tell you when I saw him sleeping under that bridge?

John Stone the cat?

Basil.

Nah.

The railroad bridge? It's high. A hundred feet if it's anything.

You never told me.

I should have.

THE BURN welled a pink face and throbbed. They stood back from the ticket booth and the front doors at the movie theater. Terry clenched a fist, yanked his sleeve down from the elbow. John Michael paced the curb, and took quick drags from a long cigarette. Neither one had money. They waited for a big enough group to get in with.

Terry passed the town's one theater often walking the town, sometimes wanted bad to go inside and watch, but he did not. Last fall he got two books of pale green grocery store stamps from his father to cash in for a ticket, but the clerk shook his head and passed them back under the window; he spoke to a long necked microphone, told him the Magic Hat Cinema of Issaqueena, South Carolina, as a strict rule, did not accept grocery stamps as legal movie tender.

He saw Alice Washington in the floodlight, close to the front of the line, by herself. She took off a pair of black plastic eyeglasses and fogged breath on the lenses and wiped them with the bottom of her shirt. She counted change and put it down to the cashier tray. John Michael went on telling him about the movie.

They build a time machine. Out of a car. A fucking DeLorean.

What's a DeLorean?

The fastest car in the world. It has doors that open up over the ceiling, like wings.

Terry picked up two torn stubs on the ground near the trash and gave one to him. A few minutes they got back of four old people, kept their faces down and went inside. He thought one usher might be wise to them. They stopped, though, for a moment at the glass counter with the candy. The machine on wheels, what looked a wheelbarrow to him, gurgled popcorn like a burst water main. Terry pulled John Michael at the jacket sleeve.

Come on, he said.

The candy here is amazing, John Michael said. They have all of it here. All of it. Fucking Sno-Caps.

She was two rows from the front. They sat a few back from her and put their feet on the chairs. John Michael got two soda cans from his jacket. Terry yanked the pull tab and tilted it. He drank half, and then he looked at Alice Washington. He looked at her some more, the back of her head, bare neck when she twisted her hair a cord, pulled it to one side and stuffed it past the neckline on her sweater. He spoke but didn't turn.

You know her? he said.

Who?

That girl two rows ahead.

John Michael crunched his eyes and poked his neck forward some, got a look at her and then settled back to the seat.

She's retarded, I think, he said.

Like the ones in the gym.

Not like those. But retarded, yes.

That's not right.

It is.

I don't believe you.

She ate like a hundred bobby pins once too. They had to pump her stomach. One Easter her class made these rabbits from construction paper, like baskets, I guess, and they put cotton balls on the outside, like the rabbit fur, you know, and that green plastic grass inside of it, and then all this candy, jellybeans, eggs, those puffy colored baby chickens, and by the end of the movie they watch she's got cotton and glue on her face, like some of that grass hanging out of her mouth. She ate all the candy, then the cotton, then the grass, then the construction paper. They had to pump her stomach that time as well, but that was before the bobby pins.

The lights dimmed. The red side curtains began to part. Terry took short pecks from the can, sipped it as he would a hot drink; white burns on the dark screen, crackle of film run through the hobbling projector.

He got up and went down beside her and held out the can. She looked at him and squinted her eyes. She shook her head, turned to the screen, and the curtain went on its high move and the dim lights. He wished to put his hand beneath her sweater and touch her bare shoulder, and then he wanted to touch her bottom lip, and then her earlobe. He did not understand these things. He leaned down and put the soda near her feet and left it.

A scientist knocked over a large sealed metal tub, and it broke open, steamed, green fluid run on the floor. The tub was top secret, controlled by a group of industrialists, and headed for the military. Terry waited for the DeLorean. One zombie with padlocks for earrings crawled from the tub and went at chewing the scientist's brain, and the scientist screamed, bewildered, and another zombie with a purple mohawk ate off his face.

Goddammit John Michael.

This isn't the one. There's been a mix-up.

Terry got his feet off the chair and leaned up, forearms at his knees.

What he thought was, where is that fucking DeLorean? The movie felt an awful, sad vision, a ridiculous thing, and worthless; the world felt less somehow, with a thing such as this movie floating around inside.

What is this shit, man?

It's just a different movie. I read the paper wrong.

An old man screamed and a group of zombies went eating on him.

I shouldn't be here, Terry said.

His body jumped.

Gross, John Michael said.

I have to leave. I can't watch this.

He looked at the back of her head two rows up.

Hang on, John Michael said.

Nah.

It was fluid.

Terry put a hand on the armrest and pushed up, turned fast, and split the aisle, the front lobby, the red guard rope, the parking lot, blacktop studded loose flagstone. The high voice of the usher, run after him like skinny dogs set loose.

8

END OF the next week the teacher stood one side of the desk and leered down on him. Terry stayed on the open math book and the teacher kept beside. He tapped the pencil at the spine, looked up, nodded quickly and put his face back down.

Teacher, he said.

A kid a few seats up spit a laugh he could not hold, put his head down at his arms on the desk. Terry turned his eyes down again. The teacher kicked her shoe at his knapsack. He turned the pencil over and erased a mark on the page, brushed the shavings. She went on the bag again. He looked up.

I didn't read last night if you're wondering that, he said.

Open your bag.

What?

I said open your bag.

I'd rather not.

Do it now.

It's personal please.

He looked at the faces turned on him. The one at his left, Richard Jenkins, looked at him and huffed. Terry studied his face and he knew.

You son of a bitch, he said.

Stand up now, the teacher said. You get sick and us too carrying that around.

Terry looked up at her.

It's not there anymore, he said.

He nodded at the bag beside the desk.

I took it out. Yesterday I did.

She raised the knapsack chest level and did the zipper. She winced and turned her head and stretched her arms long into the bag, and then she dropped it, feathers sprung from the top. She went up toward the front.

Bring it up here, she said. Now.

He got the bag at a strap and took it up front.

Take it out, she said.

He put his hand inside and got the dead bird out. He unwrapped the newspaper. It did stink.

Put it in the trash, she said.

He looked at the bird, some of its feathers gone, eyes open old black, and he felt strange, and weak. A cry bloomed in his face. He put his eyes at hers, a plead.

In the trash, she said.

The bird crunched paper falling. He looked at it there a moment, head buried, splayed on balled white.

The teacher pointed him back to his desk. He walked drop eyed, and sat down, and the cry a hard knot in his jaw. He pinched fists at the desk, looked over at Richard Jenkins, worked on some word problems like the other ones.

The bell ran loud and didn't stop. Some of the kids around him put hands on their ears. The teacher stood up front and yelled. She held a textbook above her head and squatted in front of her desk. Behind, there was a map of the Union of Soviet Socialist Republics. It was cold there. She told them the week before the Russians had a lake bigger than all the great ones up north combined and more nuclear missiles than anyone, ever, and if some important one over there just decided to, the world could end, all of them burned to cinder. They reached under the desks, to their knapsacks and got out their math books, and then they put them flat over their heads and necks and kneeled beneath the desk wood. The bell rang and kept. The teacher got from beneath her desk and stood up in front and then she pointed them to the door.

They cleared double doors, and he got Richard Jenkins near the others huddled at the back of the yard. He jammed him on a tree, pushed him up by the neck and tried to break his jaw. Then he took him down and punched on the back of his head. Richard Jenkins covered his face and his legs jerked straight at the grass. Terry hit him at the forearms, then stopped and stood over him. He felt the cry come up in his chest again and it twisted his face up. He put a hand long at his brow and over his eyes.

A trashcan, he said.

He kicked him hard. Richard Jenkins whimpered.

I was going to give it a burial, he said. A damn funeral.

He saw her stood a ways off, watching, chewing the end of a finger; he forgot Richard Jenkins huffing on the ground, felt some quick and sudden calm. He smiled a way to hide his sick front tooth and waved.

The principal got him around the chest, and another teacher came up and yanked his shirt at the front and they started to drag him. He yelled at them, hauled off, felt sad and talented, knew, from then on, he'd look for her, and that was all.

THE PRINCIPAL had a tomahawk framed on the wall behind his desk and a ball musket mounted on another, and on another were his diplomas, three of them with gold stickers and cursive signatures on the bottom, and a painting of a man fighting a tall bear with a sharp long stick and mountains behind them. Terry laughed on the sight of it, but he couldn't say why.

I never had a pet, Terry said.

Get one.

Where?

Pet store. People got dogs for free all the time.

I don't want a dog.

The principal sent him home for two days. Terry balled the pink suspension note and threw it to one of the trashcans in the courtyard.

He smoked a short joint on the way home, laughed and couldn't stop. His ribs hurt.

He sat in his room and he looked at the backyard. The leaves turned some.

10

THE NEXT day, a little past one-thirty, he waited at a piece of sidewalk downtown, the middle part of a path some kids took on the way to and from the school, old trees over the concrete, corners torn up with oak root and crabgrass. He got up behind her, and he went around to walk at her shoulder. She didn't speak, but kept walking. After a minute she turned to him and spoke.

You want something? she said.

Terry stepped to the left of a woman scuffling someplace fast, brown leather handbag held tight, in front, at her belly. He got back beside Alice Washington.

Can I walk around with you? he said.

She kept her face downturned. He blew smoke, dropped the butt and stepped it without pause, then got another and lit it.

No, she said.

Why not?

I don't need company.

He stopped on the sidewalk, cigarette in his right hand dropped close to his thigh, smoke running up along his arm, air broke, then, past his shoulder. She kept, but then she held her feet. She turned around and looked at him. She jostled her knapsack at the straps.

You come back and meet me tomorrow, she said.

Where? he said.

Over there, beside that gate.

He looked, nodded, and then she turned from him and started again on the walk. She turned while moving, spoke over her right shoulder.

Bring me some cigarettes, she said.

Alright, he said.

He watched her cross fast through the signal on Cheves, then turn left at the crosswalk.

That night Alice Washington knocked his window, and he raised the blinds, her chin at the bottom sill. She waved up at him and pointed at the latch. It didn't make much sense to him, but what he thought was, what happens when you open a window? and then he said the same thing out loud. He went over and turned the brass lock, put a hand below the pane and pulled up; slight wind, outside a new cold, and the night deep black. Lights gray and yellow white in the east, one rig and then another hitched at a box trailer, went west loudly.

They took you down the hall, he said.

You too.

That was yesterday?

It was a week ago almost.

She took off her glasses, held them an angle at the floodlight, and she put them back on. The lenses fogged some. She blinked a few times.

They took my bird, he said.

You want to go over and see his house? she said.

I don't know, he said.

Come on. They put up white candles in the yard.

She stood a few moments at the window and looked at him and then at a small white car on the highway behind. She took a pack of brand copy smokes from her knapsack and shook one to him.

She started off and then she stopped and turned back. Terry stayed at the window. She waved him again. He went to the door and jangled the knob, put a shoulder on the flat wood, leaned it hard into the frame. He sat down, bent his legs at the knees and pulled his boots on. He pushed the window open some more, hooked a leg over the frame, and then they walked in the road. Headlamps rose up behind and they went to the shoulder and the tall grass.

Basil's yard was dark, the house unlit. He looked around, saw nothing, no candles in flame, and he bit his lip and lit a cigarette, looked around some more; nothing still. Alice dipped in and out of shadows put down by the quarter moon on the trees, turned at him and held out her hand. Her fingers warm on his palm she led him to the tree, sat at the base and faced it. He fell in beside. She took a candle from her jacket and put a match to it, and then she got another and held it to him. He took it.

I got these from the church, she said. Like ten maybe. And some paper wax drip guards for your hands but those are at home. They look like the tops of umbrellas but with holes in the middle. And I lit some already. And when I said they back at your house I meant us. Me and you are the they I meant.

What are they for?

Like different holidays they have at the church.

Oh.

Holy days.

Yeah.

She looked at the ground and then to both sides. She smiled, most of it eye and cheek on one side of her face.

Groundhogs day, she said. Feast of all saints which is called Halloween but that's just so stores can sell costumes and candy to small children and rot their teeth out. Valentine's too, except that's a saint I think.

He did not understand other than she meant him to laugh softly. He did.

That's a good one, he said.

I dressed like a pumpkin this one time. I made this orange suit and stuffed it with old newspapers. I sewed green vines at the neckline.

Alright.

She leaned the flame over. He tilted his and let the wick catch. The leaves overhead stirred, some pale light scattered through.

11

O
N Wednesday Alice Washington said he looked like a younger version of a Cherokee she saw in a library book, and then she kissed him on the neck, in the stairwell closest to the vocational center, feet come down loud on the steps above them after the bell, her fingers bent on the black lacquer rail, nails bit to the quick.

TERRY DIDN'T turn all the way until she was already moving past him quickly against breezeway traffic let from fifth period classes. She gripped the chest strap at her green canvas knapsack halfway up, with two hands, fingers clenched tight, as if it were heavy rope, and she drug something behind. Sudden as highway brakes, things got mashed up, flattened, jackknifed. She ticked her shoulder and hitched the book pouch to even weight on her shoulders, flung her neck, hair tossed from the face, back over her skull. He watched Alice Washington push the right side of the double doors at the back entrance to the science building. There was a moment before the herd closed on him, a moment before he went elbow first to the walk, a space between steps. Looking at her, his body felt like wind, like the nodding broomgrass cuffed on highway shoulders; he put a hand out, and wished it to graze hers, just the fingertips, white thimbles, were enough, or the thread frayed wrist cuff on her red wool sweater. He'd give his car, all that was his, to do that, but by then Alice Washington was inside, the door closed behind her, and he watched the feet moving above him, near his face a stilt to the furrowed overhang, tall as bridge piling, hollow as rain gutter. He clutched a hand there, to raise himself up.

After class he waited, in the same spot where he fell, in the open air walkway between the vocational center and the science building, pressed a hip to one of the thin metal columns holding the roof. A cold wind sped through the wide space opened by the breezeway. He felt it through the back tail of his shirt come loose at the waist, a flap of cloth, like a bird comb, cinched above a belt loop, and crossed his arms tight over his ribs, hunched over a bit to get warm. He lifted one foot, then the other, like a horse stamping the ground when stop reined. He waited past the cars idling a bowed line on the front curb, past when the teachers left, some lighting cigarettes once out the building, even past when the custodian, a man named Smith who neared seven feet, clocked out past five, and still, he did not see Alice Washington. He went to the door she moved through, looked close at the brushed metal push handle; smudged prints the whole length of the bar. He remembered her hand at the middle, and moved his right index finger slow there, held it close for a moment, hovered just above the metal like he meant to touch coils heated on a stove, and then he put his right thumb out flat and touched the handle. It was cold, he pulled his thumb back and looked, expected some mark, a sheep brand, but there was nothing, just the same callus and dry peel, the print lines like those on a topographical map where a mountain stood. He put his thumb back to the prints; hers was there, he knew, somewhere in all the tapped hands, and then he felt it, where she passed, where her hand lingered. The bar warm, then, he put his palm open and flat against it, like one put hands to wet cement to mark the year, same as when he touched his ribs, while at rest, and felt his heart counting even time. He rubbed at it with his thumb again, but longer this time, and when he stopped, made a fist with the thumb out, put it to his mouth and suckled on it.

The old man at the service station blinked at him a few times when Terry stood at the front counter and nodded to a row of generic menthol cigarettes on the rack behind him. The old man let his feet from the bottom rung, toed the floor and stayed sat to the bar stool, four plain legs like handles from a work shovel, maroon vinyl at the padded head, two holes there patched with silver electric tape. He swiveled a half turn and reached for the cigarettes stacked deep rows, like shelved books in the library. He heard something from the radio, bayed at the sill behind him, and raised the volume, middle finger cocked to thumb. He flicked the short antennae a light three count, nail tapped against the flimsy metal. Terry kept his thumb to his mouth, took the smokes with his free hand when the old man quit the radio, got the pack and fingered the small change pocket on his jeans for two quarters.

He nodded to the penny jar beside the register when the old man held the change to him, and took a step to leave; past the door glass the night, even colder by then, and the town light, over the treeline, a yellow smudge in half moon, the glow around a gas lantern.

You got something on the end of your finger? the old man said.

Terry shook his head, but didn't speak, kept going on his thumb.

What you sucking on it like that for?

Terry shrugged, shoulders pulled up toward his ears, free hand out beside him turned open and flat to the ceiling, but still, he said nothing.

You must of put some syrup on the end or somewhat.

Terry shook his head.

Nothing?

Terry shook his head.

What you gone do when you light one of them menthols? You gone smoke through your eyeholes?

Terry shook his head. The old man lit a smoke from an open pack laid beside the register, took a pull, then leaned it to the black plastic ashtray in front of him and let it sit there, line of smoke crooked yarn between them.

It's okay. You just do what you want. I chewed on a blue blanket for twenty some years.

Terry held his left arm chest level, made a fist and stuck the thumb up, wished the sign he made to the old man to say, alright, thank you, good job, good job.

He lit a smoke, kept the thumb to his mouth and smoked at one corner, felt the smoke on his cheek, at his teeth and gumline, then run chemical through his sinus, below his eyes. He held his lips shut, and exhaled through his nose, smoke from his nostrils like church columns. What he thought was, I'm a dragon, goddammit. He pictured himself breathing fire, then his father carting a flamethrower, shoulder strapped, both of them burning towns to cinder, melted window glass sagging in the frames. He pushed his thumb back farther, until he lipped the bottom knuckle and his nose butted the backside of his hand. He kept that way; Alice Washington between his tongue and the roof of his mouth.

Later he dreamt of Alice Washington moving past him in the breezeway again and then again; he reached to touch her going past, but each time, his hand was gone, not torn, or shot off, just gone, never there to begin with, and when he woke up, three hours to first light, he'd pissed himself, and when he understood this, hands at his groin and then the sheets, he didn't care, because already, he was settled to the welt at the center of the mattress, and gone back to dream.

THE WHEELS bounced at the dirt road leading up to the white house. His father parked, the two of them walked in the grass lot, and Terry lagged at his back. Hardwick employees and their family members nicked footlines in the grass, gathered on the big front lawn, scattered paper napkins and chicken bones, voices gone loud at the trees. His father drew up with the others. The air was bright, and warm. They all wore identical orange sweatshirts made for the day, fifty-eight years since dirt broke, at their chests a black outline of the plant, as seen from the highway, a block with a smokestack, and after a while he went and stood near him. Benjamin Webber's knee popped loud like broken wood when he shifted weight. In Korea he tore some part of it, a ligament, a tendon, while carrying a flamethrower strapped to his back. The doctors sutured it ramshackle. Terry kept at two boys sitting a few feet apart in the grass, their brown hair cut to bowl lines. The elder went to the ground and picked with two hands, stuck his fingers down hard and broke grass. He raised up, moved a clod around in his hands, threw it against the other one's head, and the dirt busted, dry cloud bloomed at his face.

Going on an hour Terry stood beside him cross armed. Benjamin Webber breathed hard through his nose. His shoulders were wide and bowed. Still he was thick in the arms, and his hands were beat rough. The hair grew wiry and unkempt at the base of his neck, dark, mostly, but taken some by gray and white. Some of them talked to one another, but none came where they stood. Terry told him he was ready to go. His father shook his head.

I'm not, he said.

Come on, man.

His father turned his face down some and shook it again slow.

Just sit down or something, he said. Be quiet a little while, dammit.

I'll walk then.

Fuck you will.

Watch, then.

His father turned, looked at him square and serious.

Be fucking quiet, he said. You hear me?

I don't hear you.

He put a finger hard on Terry's chest.

You can't talk at me like that, he said. You can't.

I still don't hear you.

He got up close to Terry's face, squeezed one of his arms hard and put a finger to his chest again and shook him at the same time.

Listen, goddammit, he said.

He held Terry at the bicep and turned a few times at the others standing near and watching. Terry felt something lost in his grip, punched his chest with a closed fist, hard as he knew.

Let fucking go, he said.

For a moment his father was shaken, and then he backed him against a tree a few feet behind, put his forearm at Terry's collarbone. He pushed him against the trunk and raised him on his toes, breathed hard, eyes set. Terry turned to one side.

Just stop, his father said.

He panted.

Just stop.

He held Terry there another moment, and then his breath slowed, and his face dropped. He let him down. Some of the ones nearby kept watching. Terry swatted at them.

Yeah, yeah, he said.

He pinched his eyes and dropped his brow and put his chest out, walked stilted from all of them. He balled the orange sweatshirt he carried tightly, and threw it down a few feet ahead. He met the bundle and kicked. It caught on his toe and stuck, rose in the arc of his foot and then dropped, all the force gone at nothing, like trying to kick a birthday. He gathered it up and threw it down again, jumped on top, stomping.

He walked the edge of the place and found a graveyard through a stand of tall pine, headstones worn and broken, knee high granite. He crouched and lit a joint. The grave at his right was shaped a crib, plain baby face carved at the head. Grass filled the crib below the face. He put a hand against it flat, let it stay until the joint smoldered. He put his shoulders back against the stone, lit a cigarette, listened to the far muffled voices and shook his head at them through the trees. He dropped his eyes, circled thumbs at his temples. Seated he turned back at the crib, made scuffed dates at the head; four days, late October.

That night he slept walked, and woke chewing, taste of old ice at his tongue, refrigerator light bulb yellow on his bare feet and the wood floor. He gripped a frozen drumstick on the muscle at the fat end, ankle bone between his front teeth like a pacifier, a teething ring. He undid his fingers and turned the chicken leg the other way around and looked at it, held it up to the light come through the door, sweating in his tight grip. The skin was dimpled, colored white yellow. He had not meant to chew it, hadn't meant anything other than sleep. He did not understand what his body had set out to do without him knowing. He looked some more at the drumstick, and then he dropped it quickly to the floor, bone thud like a fallen paperweight.

T WAS a holiday. She wanted to go down by the water to a fountain she liked at one side of the park, a large marble circle like a manhole cover cut ground level, with eight spouts on the edge, water shooting clockwise arcs. She told him after the flood dropped in some houses there was a stain of waterline five feet up on the walls. She said the paper ran a detailed list of things people found in their houses; dead fish, tires, a washing machine, trees, a blue bicycle, fence posts, license plates from Indiana and Tennessee, a human jawbone with six teeth, bloated deer, mailboxes, barbed wire, a headlight, a dropped telephone pole through a first floor window, a small black bear, the hair still damp, laid on its side. One of the cemeteries, even, turned mud, and the black water raised coffins, hung them ornaments in the trees.

They timed it, moved between bursts gone overhead like the paths of electrons and stood on the wet marble, the water a gray mirror skin beneath their shoes. She kept her eyes up. The light bent through the water, and the water and the light beaded her face. She said she never saw anything like it even though she came there before.

A helicopter beat slow in the blue overhead, and carried, at its belly, hung from cord attached to the legs, a gray bridge piling. Flags limped near the water and then puffed in the wind. The silver poles waxed in the bright light, the rope joints banged against the metal.

15

THE SCREENED porch at the back of the house overlooked a runoff ditch, still water and leaves, and branches fallen and split, hunks of scrap concrete and bush grown at each lip; spring green leaves on the row, wide blossoms popped like sudden fog. He sat and pondered at the ditch, the cluster oak, late yellow leaves big as sheet maps thick in the air and splayed in the yard.

Curtis Rigby came up the steps and sat down on the porch. He wore gray pants that looked something from a space suit, four zipper pockets the length of each leg, and he was short, blue eyed, hair white blond and combed a stiff part. It looked wet, dry the same time. Terry touched a finger at the top.

What's in there?

Curtis put a hand up and patted his hair.

Leave it man. I just did this.

It's frozen or something.

Hair spray man. My sister told me about it.

What?

It's in this metal can, you shoot it all over.

He moved his hand circles at his hair.

Keeps it in place. It looks like rain or something. Mist?

What's it smell like?

I don't know, flowers or something.

You just spray it on?

Yeah.

And then your hair doesn't move?

Yeah. For like a whole day. Maybe more I've heard.

A whole day? You're making this up. Don't bullshit me.

No man. Some scientists invented it. Just recently. I'm sure there was an article in the paper. It's an important development.

I need to get some.

You can buy it at the drugstore.

Terry nodded and thumped a cigarette at the steps.

Curtis went off and he stayed on the porch and watched the dark. An air unit hummed on and kept, tires spun loud on the road when they passed the house and the floodlights put the shape of bobbed tree limbs against the wire screen. He heard children yelling on the baseball field. The lights above the backstop stayed all night.

16

AFTERNOON THEY stumbled the brick streets downtown stoned and stared at the bridge wire and steel humped over the black water. He took her hand.

Are you my boyfriend? she said.

She kept her face at the wire ties and pulled twice on the pin joint and gave it to him.

I don't know.

She blew out. The wind came hard off the river, smelled tree bark and rot.

Me neither.

You want me to?

You could. I don't like no one else.

Alright.

They found a place where Alice Washington said the old man who kept bar, greased with cataract, couldn't see who he poured to. During the daylight he never asked, because he figured the ones taking their beers before noon were old enough, by a long time, had been at nursing themselves because of children or mortgages, dead hounds and grandmothers, and wouldn't have a license, anyway, with all the wrecked cars, judges and jail cots. They put the drinking age up to twenty-one a few years before; the old man didn't know this, or he didn't much care, but either way, she said, they'd get some drinks. He followed her up to the stools, tin leg, vinyl drum skinned at the seattops, and sat down, put his feet to the low rung. He notched the soles of his boots at the angle where block heel met the arch, squashed the toes down, at the plank floor, like he pressed a gas pedal. Cigarette burns on the wood, like stress marks the reading teacher at school put above syllables on words he wrote to the blackboard. The old man got two glasses with his left hand, thumb, index and middle finger ringed at the fat handles, held them atilt beneath the beer spigot and swatted the tap with the other hand, long white hair pulled a tail in back, double knotted with a blue rubber band, the top of his hands, starting where the knuckles pressed, white, liver spots and grill burns. Terry looked at his white callused eyes, skeined wet cotton, blinking. Alice Washington handed the old man a dollar, and he nodded, rang the register door open and put the bill to the drawer.

They drank the first ones fast, then got two more and sipped at those. He felt slow, filled up a damp bog in his face and hands. Their cigarettes slumped to the black plastic ashtray, his no filters, Alice Washington's menthols, the old man bartender's skinny baby sweet cigars. Alice Washington bought two rounds for the bartender, all of them laughed there, like some family at holiday dinner.

When she kissed him, beneath the Indian head penny sign over the back door, beside a rusted grease vat, her mouth tasted sweet, his teeth slick and hard against hers, and after a minute she pulled back and studied him. She wiped her bottom lip with a back sleeve, then touched it lightly, and then she looked at the tip of her finger. She laughed, touched her bottom lip again, put the finger out to him in a point, got close to him and held it near his mouth. He let his bottom jaw sag open, her finger salty over his lips, against his tongue when she pushed it through.

It was early, dark on her street. They leaned to cars parked and squinted at the windows. Some were unlocked. They opened one and sat inside, used an ashtray in the dash. The light slipped, window glass gone frost. Her blond hair was long and wrapped on her head with a thick blue rubber band. Her glasses were too big, bent one arm from sleeping in them some nights, skin and hair streaked from never wiping them. She pushed them up on her nose. She told him she liked two rock and roll bands, Big Star and T. Rex, much more than any others. She told him she couldn't match her clothes.

She led him on the stairs, and they went to her room. He sat down on the pink shag carpet beside the bed and she went into the bathroom. She rested a hand on the sink. In the mirror at the medicine cabinet he watched her brush her teeth. She met the gums on a down stroke, used a red toothbrush with a fat head and arm. It looked something for a child. She spat loud and looked in the mirror and pulled her lips up high. She held them, clinked her teeth, spat again. The water stopped. She came back into the room and raised the lid for the record player on the low bedside table and put the arm down. The music scratched at the grooves, something he didn't know, the man's voice high, like a bird. He felt it at his hips, some wire there cut loose. He pushed up on his hands and went over and stood in front of the television. He pressed buttons at the black box on top. The channels turned. He stared at the picture. The company didn't have the means and only put wire to the edge of town, but some kids at school talked about the box with red numbers on it and all the channels and no rabbit ears. He was yet to see such a thing as cable television. She unplugged the thick wire from the back and the picture blanked. She messed with the antennae.

No one else has it, he said. Come on.

It's better you have to look for something.

I heard there's a channel that plays music, all the time, with like little movies of the songs and the bands. That's just goddamn incredible.

She put the ears wide. The picture caught, then broke up. She moved the metal around some more, turned the channel knobs. The picture stayed gray black, fast snow.

It's dumb, that television, she said.

She took an earring from her bureau, and laid it beside the antennae, and the static jumped, and popped longway at black bars run down the screen. The earring was a hoop she took from her mother, a silver crane curled on itself and biting its own feet, and she dropped it to a short white paper cup filled halfway with water and hydrogen peroxide, and she shook it around. After a few minutes she took it out, and held it over the cup. The earring dripped and bubbled.

I've seen snakes this way, she said. Feet in the mouths like that.

She pressed the tip against her right earlobe and worked it around some and pushed it through.

Not cranes though. It means something I bet.

She dipped a cotton ball to the cup, and then she dabbed her ear.

Have you done that before or something? he said.

No, she said.

Does it hurt?

Not much.

She got a picture from a dresser drawer and held it to him. He took it. A girl looked like her but older stood on a bright field, and the sky was big and deep behind her.

That's my sister Nora, she said.

He turned it over. On the back she wrote in red pen, how little we really need? and come if you want, and beneath the words a numbered state road and a box number.

She lives there, she said.

Where?

She tapped the picture.

Alice said her sister went to college nearby, dropped after three semesters, and never came back, and now she lived with some other people in houses made of wood, among evergreen and snow on ten acres somewhere north of Boulder, Colorado.

They take care of each other, she said. They grow vegetables and marijuana.

He liked vegetables and marijuana.

You can do anything you want. There's no such thing as parents.

They took a path through the woods. Seth Merritt lived in a duplex, white and plank sided, and everyone there seemed bigger than them, taller, eaters of meat and lard. Mostly they passed at shoulders, square, block jaws like the Vikings he saw on television and in the encyclopedias, flush cheeked ax wielders, beards so long and orange they twisted them to braids. He felt his face while they walked, in front of his ears where sideburns should be but were not. He rubbed his chin; something sharp, maybe, starting there. He was not sure but he felt hopeful. They went through the fireplace and cigarette smoke to the laundry room in back, and she pulled the door shut behind, and they stood quiet in the dark and listened to voices rattle the thin walls, kids from the school in the rooms past, kids who went to school there once, their sisters and people they worked with, a few bare ribbed cats. They shared a cigarette and started at a joint, and she put her face down, wiped her nose fast with the back of a hand and sniffed, spoke to him low.

Just below us now, beneath us it's concrete, and then it's dirt, and things living in the dirt, and there's rocks, and bones, and animal bones, and human bones, and past that it's more rocks, and some water, there's caves, and even farther it's the center, and it's turning all the time, and not even solid.

Terry looked at her. She kept her eyes to the floor.

Or bridges, she said. I think about those, like part will just break or crack, and cars falling off, and people in them. Or just a half bridge, and no one knows, and they keep driving. Sometimes I think I'll leave here. I was born in a car. My sister's the only one that knows that. And you now. In the backseat of a Mustang. I'm sure it was raining. I'm sure it was cold.

17

UT ON Monday she was not there. He backed to one side of the brick arch, black iron gate swung open to the courtyard, halves pushed back like unfolded box lids. When people passed on the root split sidewalk, in the new turned daylight, he dropped his chin, put his hand to the bill of his hat and nodded it to them, like he saw old men do, like cowboys on television. Some of them nodded back at him, a few smiled. He scooped one of the menthol stubs he knew she dropped, not halfway burnt, straightened the paper and filter, put it to his mouth. After he finished that one, he got another, and then he gathered up all he could find, put them to one of his empty cigarette boxes and shut the lid.

18

OCTOBER THEY rode forty miles southeast and shook cold in a grove of bone and poplar during the rain, and the wind tossed branches, and cemetery leaves hung wet in the air red and orange at the grave, and his father, somber, watched them lower his grandfather.

The way back they passed the lot she was buried, and he stayed at the car window and watched the headstones blur, and his father kept his eyes straight, yellow line past the hood.

I don't remember what she was like, he said.

You were eight months, his father said.

What was the last thing you said to her?

Goodnight.

HIS MOTHER, a tall woman, long legs skinny as dowel rods, waded into the still part of the river before the fifteen-minute break they got at nine-thirty. She was twenty, named Devin, after a great grandmother, five times back on her mother's side. She left two other women smoking at the picnic tables set in back of the plant, gave one the rest of her smokes. She took off her shoes and her clothes, folded the blue work shirt and trousers to a neat pile beside her black, ankle high work boots. The water was peat black, tinted green where light came through the high trees, littered with yellow and red leaves, and old white pollen strewn like shudders of paint. She got waist deep, kept her hands near her chest. Against her stomach the water felt rock cold, older than mountains. Then she lay back and floated that way, head up. The water moved faster a little ways down. She picked up speed, swept quick with the water like a branch dropped, fluttered hands at her sides, legs straight and long, feet up, soles at the rocks, and then she was at the smaller of the two falls, bouncing through. She went over the big drop, before the boat lock, before the dam, and went under for good.

Of his mother, Terry remembered waking slowly, as if there was no dark, only slow lumbering through morning half light; he remembered morning smelled of pine resin. He remembered the red divots on her temples and cheeks from the tight band on the work goggles she wore most day hours. Nothing else.

2 0

H E SAW a blue one at the hardware priced three quarters, knit, like the red hat he wore to think. He didn't have words for that sort of blue. Blue like the monster on television that ate cookies, eyes on top of its head, blue like the world close to first light, globe ocean blue. He stuffed it to the front of his dark jeans. The store was owned by an old man who was often kind to him, and on the way out he waved at him and the old man waved back. Terry kept his hands in the deep pockets and pushed them forward against the cloth and held the jacket shut at the front metal zipper and the buttonholes over his chest and waist.

When he thought on it, in the afternoon and later again in the night, he felt small, that he led a petty life. But he wore it the next day past dark, and it made his forehead itch, and he scratched at it through the cloth, and when he pulled it off before he slept his hair stood up high one side and mashed on the other, and his forehead was streaked red scratch lines.

Later he woke in the room dark, some pale light from the hall, and he needed water, his tongue bound at his teeth and the roof of his mouth, his eyes gunked at the corners. He went into the kitchen and ran the tap, drank two glassfuls, and then he turned the water hot and put some at his eyes and rubbed them. He passed the den, woodland triptych over the brown couch slightly cocked to one side, and stopped, backed and stood at the empty frame, the molding at his head wood colored and squared. His father lay at one side with his knees pulled close to his chest. His head nudged the brick on the floor. A nodded low flame lit one part of his face.

The coals wept orange and the fire moved inside them, and the embers hissed, and popped, and one leapt a high arc and skidded at the wood floor, settled and kept bright hot in the dark, and then another coal spat but was dead before it struck the wood. He looked closer, blinked at the dark and the flame tilt shifting light in the room. He saw thimble holes burned at the floor in other spots. He bent down and put hands to them, and then he stooped behind his father. He sat down and prodded one hand on his wide back, and he shook him, and then he patted the top of his head, hair sprigged thin and white on top, his scalp pink, shined wet in the light put there by the fire. He kept his face to the coals. A few minutes Terry sat and watched him breathe, and blink, and smoke held at the flue and fell back a skein and high in the room. Terry's eyes watered. He lit a cigarette and took a deep pull, and then he put it to his father's lips, and he drug on it, and blew out. Terry stood up, finished the smoke in two pulls and thumped it to the coals. He nudged his father at the back with one foot and then he did it some more.

You going to get up? he said.

No. I'm not.

He reached under the top rim of the fireplace brick and jostled the lever on the flue. He felt the air draft up the chimney. He sat again behind him.

You should sometime, he said.

I can't.

Alright.

He left the house and tramped the yard toward the treeline, and the light sifted gray in the east. He stopped past the first of them and then he stood beneath an old tall oak and looked up on it, deep lined trunk, leaves bobbed animal. What he thought was, you can't be. What he thought was, you won't hold. A few minutes he turned the questions in his head and meant to sort them, but then his father stood beside, eyes red and smelling ash, his arms crossed high at the chest, wearing a blue robe and old knee high duck boots untied. He wore a tall, round boxed hat just onto his deep lined brow, brown fur, black flecked on the ends, animal pelt, soviet.

Where did you get that hat? he said.

I won it.

For what?

I can't remember. It was a long time ago.

What is it, like a beaver or something?

It's grizzly bear.

Really?

No. It's antelope.

Really?

No.

Well what is it?

I'm not sure.

Terry looked at him. What he thought was, what kind of man are you? He passed him the lit cigarette, and got another. He didn't know a thing about him. They smoked, and did not speak, watched the tree and the coming light. His father reached a few feet up the trunk, held a bundle of gray moss one hand, worked it apart some with the other.

2 1

NOVEMBER THEY ditched for a pool hall close to noon. He sat with Alice Washington in a booth at a back corner, and they watched old men and old women at the bar smoke cigarettes and lean over their drinks. Lightning caught up in far off clouds through the tall windows. The tables in the place were silent, chairs keyed at four sides, cues racked on the walls, and the air old chalk in the table lights.

He said how he liked to watch a storm come up. He said he liked how all the trees got caught and leaned, and how the stiff neck pine shook tall in a storm, how it reached. He told her how he saw lightning take a bird in flight, the white line come up from the ground and the bird, not dropped, or split, just gone. He told her a bird was as much a part of the sky as a cloud. He said, the sky takes things back, just like the water, or the ground. He said, all of them want something lost.

22

B ENJAMIN WEBBER was home when Terry came in, shifts cut for half the month. He pointed at the ceiling in the front room. A hummingbird beat green and red at one corner and knocked at the plaster face first, stuttered back and lunged again on the same spot and did not stop.

It'll die, his father said.

So what?

Terry went and got a yarn dust broom from the closet. He came back and his father opened the front door. Terry held the broom at the ceiling and huddled the bird, and then he didn't see it anymore. He lowered the broom some at the handle and then he saw the bird caught in the dust and the red yarn. He rushed at the door and shook it past. The bird shot a green spark over old leaves in the yard.

He left the house and walked around in the woods. He sat in a rusted bathtub at a clearing and splayed his feet. He smoked, held his arms up, made like he worked soap on his chest, in his hair.

He walked to the sporting goods, brushed his fingers at tennis balls in skinny cans and wooden racquets on the first aisle, soccer balls and wood bats and baseballs and gloves at the next one. He stopped on the guns two rows over and put his hands on the case glass with the rifles and the shotguns and the scopes behind, the boxed shells and bullets shelved beside, and then the bird calls arranged past those, and then the doe rut, and then the decoys. The pellet guns and slingshots were stacked at the end of the aisle. He held one of the displays, rifle shaped, tied with plastic theft cord to the shelf. He aimed it on the ceiling, and then he put it back. He took one, heavy black plastic, held his arm straight and sighted a decoy on the shelf, a wood duck, eyes cat yellow and bright. He checked both ways and lifted the front of his shirt, put the gun to his belt, and then he looked at the air pellets, took a box of a hundred and dropped it to a pocket in his green army jacket, and then he left the store. The pellets rattled in the box.

He got halfway, and then he turned back. The gun jostled some at his beltline. He pushed it back tight when he saw the sporting goods, waved at the store clerk inside and walked slow again at the gun aisle and tried to remember the space where the box of pellets fit and when he found it he took the box from his jacket and set it there.

He came back in two hours, and Benjamin Webber sat at the table in the kitchen. He worked one bottom corner on a puzzle and rummaged loose pieces. He picked one up, and then he turned it over, put it to other pieces laid out. The box was on the floor. On the lid there was a sharp color picture, at the center of it a statue, steel colored, one man pointing, another slack armed next to him. The plaque beneath was labeled THE COMING OF THE WHITE MAN. Yellow leaves piled at the stone base and tall city buildings loomed behind, sky heavy gray and cold. He tried another piece and dropped it. He rubbed his eyes and blinked hard. He stood up, limped over to the blinds and pulled them, the table lit some in the daylight. He was barefoot. The duck boots lay on their sides under the table. He soaked his right heel, rust colored from part of a bottle cap lodged there, in a cereal bowl filled with bleach. He'd stepped on it in the yard five years back, taking trash out barefoot, at night. He pried most of it out with his fingernails, but part of the bottlecap was stubborn, stuck deep in his heel, and once he started working at it with his penknife, he understood it took more of him to get it out than to just leave it be.

That's a hard puzzle it looks like, Terry said.

I've been at it a week.

What kind of statue is that?

I don't know.

He looked at the picture on the puzzle box.

Those are explorers.

His father looked too.

They had to eat candles because they ran out of food. I read that. I think it's the same ones.

His father studied the picture, face close.

They look younger than me, he said.

Terry went to his closet and took the gun from his belt and put it to the pocket of a plastic apple green raincoat. He fumbled the top rack for the red snow hat.

He came back into the kitchen and dropped the hat in front of him on the table. His father picked it up with one hand and looked at it hard, turned it inside out and then back again.

I haven't seen snow for a long time, Benjamin Webber said.

He pulled the bottom to the crown of his head, tin gray hair jutted from the sides.

It's red, Terry said. For thinking. I got a new one.

Like this?

Further down. Closer to your eyes. It has to be on good. You have to warm up your brain.

He thought this was true, but he was not certain.

It helps me usually, when I can't figure something.

He pulled the hat down closer to his eyebrows. He put his face back down at the puzzle, sorted a few pieces to a pile.

I shouldn't have gone at you so hard the other day, he said.

Doesn't matter.

I get scared sometimes, he said.

Down the hallway yellow light pushed the bottom slit of his bedroom door shut.

I'm scared of things I've never seen.

Yeah, Terry said. The Russians keep me up at night. Or just wars, I guess.

This air raid siren used to ring all the time when I was young. It hurt my ears. The teachers made us run home from school. I was waiting for a plane, or a bomb falling. This one lined us up at the door, said, go fast, don't look up.

All night he sat at the table in the kitchen with his hands on the wood in front. He thumbed the puzzle pieces. He picked callus skin on his hands beneath the fingers and shifted the weight on his back and shoulders. He smoked cigarettes and dropped them at a soda can on the table, watched the black and white television on the counter. The picture struck light on his face and in the room. He cut at the table with a kitchen knife from the drawer, dusted the wood shaving. His head felt a jumbled mess, but he couldn't figure why. He went to the closet and got the gun from the raincoat.

23

HE TURNED the engine near the guardhouse. Mostly dark still he watched the sun come big and torch red at the top of the black tupelo and the sumac crowned a short red dirt bluff. He watched the light steam hard frost on the grass where the shadow did not reach. The guard came up the gravel drive and parked the car. She shut the door and then got back inside and turned off the headlamps. She pushed the door shut again and went over to the small watch booth and turned the light on inside. She saw his car and came out of the booth and stood there past the door and squinted her eyes at him. He cracked the window a slit and stuck his hand out and waved. She came over beside. He rolled it the whole way down, took the cigarette from his mouth and leaned it to the ashtray. He smiled.

Early, she said.

He nodded, and then he got the cigarette up and took a pull.

I got a project, he said. A school report.

On what?

History. Battles and all what.

This was true. One was due two weeks before.

She put a hand at her brow for the glare and scanned the backseat.

On the general, he said. That Pickens one.

She looked him straight for a long moment and squinted her eyes. He tapped the white paper near the ash. She raised up all the way and stood there.

He was an Indian killer, she said. Write that in your report.

He nodded. She put her eyes away from him then and to the main road and shook her head. She jostled the brass and silver keys at the circle ring laced on a beltloop and went over to the gate and undid the padlock holding the heavy chain. She went back inside the guardhouse. He drove slow on the early wet road and put the window down, waved at her gone past.

The woods cut to a field past the gate, and he stayed at the dirt road and followed a half circle, and it turned to woods on both sides then ended at another field. He parked the car and got out, stood at a thick wooden sign like a pulpit, the name of the general cut on top, and the name of the fight below that, shot buried pinholes on the face. He thought about those tablets in church that the old man came off a mountain with. They seemed good rules. No killing or stealing, something like that. He put cigarettes out on the sign and dropped the ends to a front pocket. He kicked burst shells, twenty or more.

The grass was high, white brown in the new cold, and rocked in the stiff wind. He walked a straight line through the middle, and the grass shook thick and bent under his boots, and he put his hands at the tops and ran them over.

He heard the fight in the trees, chatter left in the grass, the dust of felled houses and the quickly dead, first names, a hope for child.

He sat down, wind in his ears and eyes watered on the dry air.

The bright cold stayed in the afternoon and he drove and kept the window down and smoked the rest of the joint. He slowed at the exit to his highway and then turned on. Three police cars sat each shoulder gone to the crest, their sirens spun blue and red. There were german shepherds yelling. Officers held them at chains. He rolled the window halfway and then he was between them.

One asked why he took that particular exit. Another stood beside him pressing buttons on a hand held radio. He said certain numbers into one end.

It's my exit, Terry said.

The one with the radio asked for his address. Terry told him.

It's not your exit.

It is, he said.

It was his. He used it a few times already. The officer told him to get out of the car.

Where's your adult? he said.

Sixteen was the age for unaccompanied driving.

He put his hands on the back of his hips and spit because sometimes he liked to spit.

The policeman put Terry's face against the roof of the hatchback and mashed his lips down until spit ran.

This is bullshit, he said. I know that.

They pulled his arms behind. The one at his head pumped his face down on each word.

Shut the fuck up, right now, he said.

Inside his car a dog whined.

Okay, okay, goddammit, okay, I understand.

He didn't understand, not even a little.

He spit blood in the kitchen sink. His bottom lip was fat and felt stiff when he poked it. He pulled his father's whiskey from the cabinet, held it up in front and in light over the sink, sloshed the brown whiskey in the bottle. He drank a mouthful and washed it around. His eyes watered. He heard car engines running full out and hot, smelled burnt tire, felt gasoline at his nose, and in his cheeks. He stomped his feet. He spit again and yelled something, head lost on how much it burned. He punched the pantry door and left knuckle marks.

N THE gas station he stood at the pay counter beside a stand of menthol cigarettes and kept his busted hand to a pocket. His lip welled. He felt his heartbeat in it and then at his neck. The old man cashier kept at his newspaper and drank coffee from a short white paper cup. Terry heard a bell. The old man hunched forward and pressed a yellow button to start a pump.

He got a bottle of aspirin and two green and white packets of headache powder near the end of one aisle, soda from the cooler in the back, and he put them in his jacket. He saw a rich man named Nola Walker up front, standing, leaned elbows at the front counter and talking to the old man. He owned the junked car field and the dirt bike track, the textile mill where his father worked. He was the one that sold him the blue hatchback. Terry conjured the Bengal tiger pouncing and then eating Nola Walker. He conjured the howler monkey dancing on Nola Walker's chest and banging a small tambourine.

Terry went back to the front of the store. He fingered a felt bag of polished rocks at a display shelf. Some of them came from mines, some were sifted from river dirt. He untied the string on top of the sack and held the rocks out and studied them. Some were green, some pink, some white and swirled. He moved them around in his palm, closed his fingers over.

Nola Walker pushed the door and went outside. The newspaper creaked a fold, again the gas bell. He checked at the cashier, stuffed two bags to his jacket with his good hand, and then he opened the door and hopped the curb.

His breath fogged. Nola Walker was near the pumps, leaned beside a tire. Terry walked fast, rocks clicking, jostled in his pockets on the aspirin and the soda. He put hands to quiet them, turned again on the rich man. Nola Walker raised up from the tire and glared hard at Terry, pinched his eyes a slit. Terry put his face down at the lot and went faster. He stopped and turned at him when Nola Walker yelled.

What? he said.

Nola Walker kicked the rubber hard, made steps at him and bore his eyes. Terry felt the air a high cold in his ears and at his head. Nola Walker looked at the holes worn white string at Terry's knees.

Your momma can't buy you any good pants? he said.

My mom hasn't bought me pants in a long damn time.

You took something in there, he said.

Terry shook his head and didn't say anything. He took hands from his pockets and held them up.

See? he said. I got nothing.

You think I'm dumb?

No.

He felt the bags in his jacket against his ribs.

Take it back, Nola Walker said.

I didn't take anything.

You did.

You don't even know me.

I know what you look like boy.

Not your boy.

Terry put his eyes on the ground, and then back up.

You've got mange I bet, Nola Walker said.

Terry scratched one side of his head.

Whatever that means, he said.

He hated Nola Walker, his ridiculous and shined new truck, raised high on show tires, spitting gray from the pipes. He hated his glossed brown shoes with tassels on them. He hated his white pressed shirt. He hated his cursive initials on the cuffs. He hated his pretty fucking hands.

You don't know a goddamn thing, Terry said.

Is that right?

Nola Walker pointed at him and took a step toward.

You like the police, he said.

I don't even want these rocks.

Nola Walker turned from him and took a few steps toward the filling station; Terry's head went hot, and light, and he could feel all his ribs, forearms beating, he didn't know what else. He reached behind, at his belt, and pulled the empty gun. He held it low at one side, where Nola Walker could see, and spoke loud.

Right there goddammit.

Nola Walker held and turned around.

What?

I'm going to shoot you in the head.

Nola Walker looked at the gun stuck out and then he stayed at Terry's face. He put up his hands. Terry took a big step, poked the barrel at him high and shoulder level. Nola Walker's head dropped some, face scrunched in what looked a cry.

Don't fucking move, Terry said. I mean it. Turn around.

He kept his hands up and turned his back slow to Terry.

Keep that way.

The back of his head went a nod and Terry kept the nose on him.

Come on now. I won't say anything. I won't.

Start counting goddammit.

He nodded again and whimpered the first number.

Terry put the nose at the back of his head, the dip where neck met skull, and he pressed it hard. His back raised and bent with his fast breath. On his stuttered number five Terry pulled the trigger. The hammer clicked dull plastic. He felt Nola Walker clench and then stop counting. He kept the gun.

Keep going, Terry said.

Nola Walker started crying faster, and more.

I guess you better pray if you do that sort of thing.

He got slow to twelve; again, Terry pressed the trigger.

Terry ran from Nola Walker and the parking lot and didn't stop until his ribs screamed a cramp. He stopped at a small bridge over a creek. He took the gun from his pocket and bobbled it, and it fell at the ground, and he bent and gathered it up, swept dirt from the rough handgrip. He held it an arm over the water, and then he pulled it back. He took the jacket off, used one sleeve as an oven mitt and wiped it down. He held it over the rail and let it fall on the black water.

He woke flatback near a small table and no light in the room. Head stilted, he wore his jacket still. The rotary phone shook at a ring and feet stomped the wood near his head. His eyes dumb at the quick dark, he blinked hard. The phone slammed, the plastic base cracked. He blinked again. His father paced the room to the front door and went out to the backyard.

Terry slapped his cheeks one at a time, wagged his head and got to his elbows. He went over to the window and looked out to the yard, night wet, a yellow tint. His father lifted a shovel and swung it high through a floodlight and down. The square head cut the dirt. He was not digging, but wanted only to hit something hard. He did it once more, then left the wooden handle and walked rings around it and panted steam. Sweating in the cold dark Benjamin Webber looked the leftovers of a dogfight. Terry slouched below the window, back to the wall. His head went a waking dream; a bear sat nearby in the room and turned at him, and the two locked eyes. Outside the engine turned, wheels backed fast on the drive.

FOR TWO days the river ran a high flood in the woods between John Michael Johnson's house and the small bridge where the interstate crossed above the water, and then it shrank back some, and left things stranded. The metal boat fit two, but John Michael said it could hold three of them. He, Terry, and Curtis, together, didn't weigh too much, and he did it before, not long ago with his older brother, a hairy, giant man named Turbeville. The boat sat flipped over in the work shed near some open paint cans. There was an orange riding lawnmower a few feet off, two plastic jugs of gasoline nudged at the wheels. Leaned to the wall beside he saw yard tools; a pair of hedge clippers, wood handle duct taped at the grips, metal shears a curved beak on top; hoe, spade, stump shovel, rake with blue comb rusted at the tips; all of it layered dust and cobweb. There was a work counter at the back; a mounted vise clamp, nails and screws and bolts and washers in a slide drawer box, cuts of sandpaper, a blue and orange instant coffee tin used as an ashtray, two cans of industrial lubricant for greasing metal parts, pumice soap in a gallon press dispenser.

On the long shelf above the counter there was an old radio, a clock, two bottles of castor oil, and a mason jar with what looked a large kidney bean floating inside. He went over close and picked it from the shelf. It was a heart, a small one, wafted in clear, heavy liquid. He asked, and John Michael told him he pulled it from a duck, a mallard he helped his father and grandfather clean about six years before. The pharmacist downtown gave him formaldehyde for the jar so the heart would keep a long time. Terry put the heart back on the shelf. Tacked on the naked beam walls were pages cut from department store catalogues of women in bras, black and red and pink. Curtis stared at one, bright leaf green.

I can see this one's nipples, he said. They're really big. Like drink coasters or stars or ferris wheels or something.

Curtis put a finger against the cutout and held it there.

I'd cut off my pinky finger if this one would let me see her titties. And I could give her my boner.

Your boner? John Michael said.

My dipstick.

You'd cut off your pinky?

Give me a hatchet.

Have you seen Jessica's?

Through her shirt. But she won't take it off. I wish she'd let me play with them sometime.

Her titties?

Her nipples and her titties. I can tell they're big. Both of them.

They turned the boat over and carried it outside, through the back field and to the start of the woods and the old hunting road, and then they dropped it, huffed a moment at the work and caught their breath. It was too heavy to carry the whole way like that, a mile at least on the path before the shrinking waterline. John Michael latched a rope he tied at the bow on two hands, hung part of it over one shoulder and drug the boat behind him. Curtis walked and pushed at one side, Terry at the other, and the ground got softer the farther they walked, and soon it was pluff and mud, and they stopped, turned the boat upside down and sat on top to rest again. Terry took a new pack from his bag and gave one to each of them. Curtis lit his cigarette with a silver army lighter, butane swathed his face when he snapped the top cap open and drug his thumb over the flint and the wick caught. The high water turned the ground compost, pine needle and brown leaf mashed to a thick veil, and left fish behind, yards of them it looked, endless, gray as brains.

Your mom's got nice legs, John Michael said.

John Michael stood up, hopped between fish, put a toe against one colored pewter and poked it.

I bet she runs a lot.

John Michael kicked the fish then. It broke in two pieces, at the gills.

Don't say that, Curtis said.

John Michael held a small one head up, gray tail jutted from the fist.

I'm just saying, he said. I bet she runs. Fast, man, and often.

Curtis stooped over and put his hands against his knees, dropped his face, huffed a sigh. He stood up from the boat, walked at the trees grown thick past the edge of the path.

Hey man, John Michael said. Hey.

Curtis hopped a fallen tree, then they couldn't see him anymore.

Where's he going? John Michael said. It's all woods.

He went a step in the direction Curtis took and yelled after him, hands cupped a lampshade at his cheeks.

You'll get lost man, he said.

He stopped and looked for a moment at the trees, yellow pine and sycamore, yaupon holly thrush red at their trunks, and then he turned back, long strides, like a stilt walker, sopped and loud when his boots raised from the peat.

They burned most of the short cigar Terry cut in the middle, dope twisted in with the tobacco, a few shards of hash John Michael got from the pocket of Turbeville's aviator jacket. With the smoke the woods got clear edged, trees singled and named, and some of the fish gasped. He wondered if he could eat them and he wondered how to catch one in a river. He wondered what they were before they were fish, and then he wished he had gills on his neck. He thought to find a dragonfly and eat it. They waited on Curtis to come back, but he didn't.

He'll catch up, John Michael said.

They got to either side and flipped the boat. John Michael went up front to the pull rope. Terry pushed at the back end. Soon the hash let off some in his head and the water got higher on the ground. A fish landed out front, and a few moments later another went near John Michael's feet, and then they came faster. The eighth fish caught John Michael on the ear. He stumbled and the rope dug on his shoulder and came loose. The weight of it spun him around. His finger hold gave and he let go and the bow dropped and splashed river on his back. He put a hand on the ear and grimaced. Terry stumbled forward, and caught himself with his hands on the gunnel and stood right. He saw Curtis in some trees on the far side behind them. Curtis gathered up another fish and tossed it overhand at John Michael.

Quit, please? John Michael said.

Another fish and then another struck his back.

Those are your issues, man, not mine, John Michael said. I've got my own ones, man.

The fish, then, flung handfuls, like dropped nickels.

I'm sorry, I'm sorry, John Michael said. I'm sorry, okay, I'm sorry.

Do you mean it? Curtis said.

John Michael shook his head and didn't say anything. Curtis scooped another fish and pegged it sidearm. John Michael put his forearms up and winced.

I mean it man, he said. I swear. I won't say things about your mom anymore.

Curtis dropped the fish readied at his hip.

You know it bothers me, he said.

I know, John Michael said. I'm sorry, like I told you man. I won't do it again.

Do you swear?

Yeah. Yes, dammit.

People said things like that often about Curtis's mother. Terry knew he was tired of hearing them. She was good looking the way they were in old movies, had a boyfriend seven years younger who taught guitar lessons and played lead in a Rush cover band. Curtis hated him, even though he was kind and well meaning, because his father was dead in Korea or somewhere, but he wasn't sure exactly. Curtis never knew him, not even a minute, but conjured him some valiant soldier fighting communists.

Just don't anymore, he said. Alright? I have to hear that shit all the time.

Okay. I won't.

John Michael got the rope again and stretched it at his shoulder and started pulling the boat. Terry got back at one side and Curtis went to the other.

The water welled at their knees, and then it was on their waists. They sat in the boat, pushed the ground with a split oar until they floated beneath the overpass, sun red over the guardrail, water glassed beneath the full leaves, the flooded oak, sumac, and gum. John Michael pointed the binoculars up, at the tails of cars passed west on the interstate, and he read their license tags out loud. For a few years he catalogued plates, had twenty-four of them so far. The hardest ones to spot, he said, were states in the upper midwest, Minnesota and the like, and then Idaho, and Wyoming, and Montana; he wanted Nebraska, badly.

Ohio, he said. Delaware. Virginia. Goddamn South Dakota. I've got all these. South Carolina. South Carolina. North Carolina. South Carolina. Dammit. South Carolina. North Carolina. North Carolina. North Carolina. Motherfucker.

I need to bone Jessica real bad, Curtis said. I mean it. She smells like jelly donuts.

Would you shut the fuck up? John Michael said. I'm counting tags here.

John Michael let the binoculars hang at his neck. A leak came on at the boat head and dribbled water at the floor.

They left the boat at the edge of the woods, amongst thick shrub, black-haw and guelder rose, below beech and sourwood branched thick overhead. John Michael stole his sister's keys inside, from the newest place she hid them, balled inside a red scarf on the closet shelf above the coat rack. He left a note there that read checkmate, bitch. They went fast in her car and put the windows down. They stayed in the wet clothes and pushed glass double doors, and the air was food locker cold, and his shoes put wet spots on the grocery tile. They thumbed cleaning supplies both sides of aisle four, bleach, detergent, and sponges, plain and bristled, and air freshener in metal cans, spring mist, country garden, winter pine. They argued brand and taste and the foam made inhaling. Curtis liked the foam, said it tasted like candy flowers, but Terry didn't much, and neither did John Michael. They took four cans labeled Country Garden. Curtis got one called Cinnamon Holiday, put the top close to his nose and breathed in hard.

It tastes like Christmas, he said. Reindeer. Colored lights. Pecans. Pine trees. They got washrags at John Michael's house and draped them over the spouts, put one hand beneath the cloth and pressed the nozzle, used the other to hold the cloth tight, and the spray filtered through it, white pink at their lips, fumed in their throats and in their brains.

John Michael faced a long mirror on back of his bedroom door, moved a robot gait, white foam on his mouth, and Curtis lay on the floor beside the bed, empty can fell near a shoulder, another rested on his belly, washcloth over his mouth pushed with his breath. The fumes sat in Terry's head a slow hum, rose a wave and went to flatline, soldered him crosslegged and pinned eye, shoulder blades hard on the closet door.

Next day the light outside came early on the house and he pushed the window shade a slit. He watched his father open the passenger side door and put a blue duffel bag into his car. He came back to the front steps and picked up a cardboard box and carried it over. He got another one, and then another. Terry coughed at a fist, lit a cigarette and knocked ash into a soda can on the sill. His mouth tasted rosewater, and petals, teeth still foam slick. He tore a page from a beat up school notebook, spiral blue, marked history and his first name, and folded it five ways to an airplane. He tossed it a crooked line to the ground. He went to the desk again and knocked scrap paper at the floor, opened the lock drawer and got one of the felt bags he took at the filling station. He shook the rocks inside. They clinked small, sounded like marbles or necklace beads. He went over to the window and threw one at his father's car. It landed short and jumped the dirt, and the next fell the same, and the next skidded on the drive. He threw a few more, and then he dropped the rest slow over the frame, to the grass, and then he flicked the bag, and then at the desk he got the other bunch, tied still, and let it fall. His father cranked the car, and it puffed when he put it to gear and sputtered at the tailpipe. He looked once over his right shoulder and backed out.

DECEMBER SCHOOL let for holiday. Her parents found an open pack of menthols in her knapsack and put her in the house for two weeks. He stayed at his room, and he watched the streets, and at night he went out with a wooden bat, and split a wooden cut out of a coal eyed snowman with a red scarf, and he went for a reindeer at the front of a sleigh, antlers glistened with snow paint, busted two candy canes, and then he backed his car at a yard tree strung with colored lights, yanked a bundle and held, punched the gas, and the lights tore from the tree. He trailed a long rope of them and the wire flapped at his windows in the cold air passed, and he opened his hand, and let it go at the street.

THEY SAT crosslegged, past where floodlamps from her house lit the grass yellow, on top of two small mounds at the center of what looked six or seven in a row, the rear section of her backyard where she buried old pets. There was a wire post fence separating them from twelve acres owned by an old man, Foncie Allen, who in his old age leased his fields to soy farmers, let them build drums to house the beans, set deer corn in fall and kept peacocks all year. They heard them gurgling in the dark, baby clicks, tail fans open and shut.

Drink it, Alice Washington said.

Terry got two bottles for a dollar and thirty-one cents, four cigarettes.

You do it, he said.

That stuff's nasty, she said.

Terry held up one of the bottles, wrapped with foil at the mouth instead of a plastic cap. Inside looked dirt shaken, flakes spun behind glass in a snow globe.

Is not, he said.

You drink it then, she said.

He looked inside again, then he let it down near his lap and took the foil off, held it to his nose, turned it up. He meant to swallow quick, keep his nostrils locked, but the drink was strong once at his tongue, it welled up in his face and clenched his throat. He spit the mouthful near his feet.

They won't stop with those hammers, she said.

Who?

Them.

She pointed to the framed tudor at the new cleared lot north of their property line. He stood up with her, they walked over and toed the yard, all dirt, a long narrow green bin for the site forklifted there, foundation mounds, two of them, beside the open air carport. They got inside, over the railing, stood on cardboard boxes broke down at the folds, stacked leaves, roving nails, shingles, and drywall, flush valves, copper pipe fittings, supply lines and wall spigots, blazed newsprint at their faces. They sat down and smoked and sometimes put their hands to the box flats. The ink stained their hands. Alice Washington looked at hers and rubbed them together. She looked again. It was worse, smudged with more ink. She laughed, and leaned over. She looked at his slight jaw, then to his forehead, pox marks at his brow, and kept her eyes there. She brushed his hair back some, combed a sweep at his bangs with the end of one finger. She looked at him some more. He thought to say something, tell her she smelled like pink shampoo, that most of the time he wanted to lick her face. Sometimes, too, he wished to lick her arms. Sometimes he wanted to suck on her fingers.

Could you be still with me? she said. When everything else is so loud I fall down?

He nodded.

Will you run if I show you mine?

I won't, he said.

28

WEDNESDAY NIGHT he came back and stood in front of the fireplace. He held a section of wood knocked from a reindeer in someone's yard. It was the red nose, part of an eye. He thought whether or not to put it on the fire. His father pushed the front door, went past him to the kitchen, came back after a moment and sat the couch. He pointed to the torn wood.

Where's that from?

Terry held it up and looked down at it.

I found it, he said.

Yeah?

In the road.

He squatted on his heels in front of the fire and laid it in. It caught after a few minutes. The paint burned off red and chemical and glowed the flame. He stayed a crouch and watched it go, and then his father spoke behind him, and Terry stood up, and turned around. His father rubbed his hands, and went slow on telling him; he got a new job, at a plant in a town called Echota, three and some hours east. He didn't know when they had to leave. He waited on word from the new manager.

Sometime past new year, he said. I'll let you know when I do and then we'll have a couple of days to get things together.

Terry nodded.

It doesn't matter, Terry said.

He remembered four times. They moved so much, passed people and towns like a rumor most of the time he couldn't tell the difference between staying or going.

What's wrong with the job you got now? he said.

It's not there anymore.

29

THIRD FULL week the town hung lit ornaments at the end of bridge lamps; blue and red, white and green fat colored bulbs, shaped candy canes, snowmen, reindeer. He stopped at the crest, and looked over the side to the black water steel and cold. He spit, wiped his mouth with the back of a sleeve. The stoplight at the foot of the bridge blinked; the downtown behind dark then drawn red in the throb.

Dusk he left the station where Deaccus and King crossed at a yellow light and thumped a pack of cigarettes topside against a palm. He stopped at the curb and spit, sat down and let his feet on the road. He studied an old house on the northwest corner, pink at the front, white on the rest, clapboard shutters at the windows green and open, front door mismatched wood and small for the frame. The yard was dirt, one side of the front porch stacked with tires. Guinea hens pecked and kicked around the steps and at the yard and the walk. An old pig white at the jaw nosed the yard and wore a Christmas wreath at the neck, bells sewn into the green, rang dull when it waddled. An old woman lived in the house. On the east side of the place an empty firework stand built for holiday shouldered more tires and the shells of cars and a spring bed frame, a stove, a septic tank, stacks of cinder block and brick and old pipe. The old woman poked the yard, leaves in her hair and on her clothes. She tossed seed to a cloud of hens, put a hand to the old pig's mouth. The pig licked her hand, and she patted its back, and scratched at the ears. Her mailbox was labeled KEHOE.

He watched his father step from the car and walk toward the filling station with keys and folded bills in one hand. He limped at his back heel. A few minutes passed. He came back out and got into the car and shut the door. Terry made across the lot, stood next to the car and knocked the window with a fist. There were boxes stacked in the backseat, a pile of clothes on hangers laid long on top. He saw his shoulders and his head stretched long in the glare from halogen on glass. He looked hard, then turned down to his lap. He cranked the car, and looked up. The window fell. Terry looked at him for a moment, and then he cocked his head at the backseat.

It's late boy, his father said.

He looked over the roof of the car, turned his eyes over the lot.

We going to leave soon?

A few weeks. A month. Something.

Terry shifted weight from one hip to the other.

Come back to the house when you get tired of walking around, Benjamin Webber said.

Alright.

You know how things are so nasty and pretty you want to fall over sometimes? I know about that. I do.

He drove off, and Terry stood there and smoked. A man who worked inside held the door and yelled at him.

Get the fuck away from the pumps.

Terry didn't understand. He spit.

You're going to start a goddamn fire boy.

He took a pull, and looked at the cigarette.

Yeah, alright, alright. Fuck alright.

He stepped what felt a safe distance. The attendant went back inside the station and let the door shut.

A crash of feather and teeth then in the yard of the old house. One pack dog came up in the yard and took two birds, and then more of them gathered and snarled and held twitching guineas in their mouths. They moved jagged circles and worked on the last hens, pink mawed, full of feather and tiny bone. One went for the pig, snapped at its hind legs and chased it around the yard. The bells rang on its neck wreath. Its cries were desperate, clueless.

Terry picked up a handful of gravel beside a dumpster, heavy in the palms, and he ran to the dogs, the birds, and the wailing pig. He threw the rocks hard and straight, worked on the dogs one at a time. Some turned and jostled away. A few moaned.

The pig stuck its nose about the ground and jawed the scraps of birds after the pack left. His heart beat fast. One of the dogs circled and came back. It bore teeth, and studied the pig nudging the ground, stayed half in shadow at one side of the firework stand and moved in and out of the dark. The boy got a piece of scrap metal at the ground. He held it at a sharp end and pushed the tip on the dog.

You want a fight? That it?

Things got confused in his head; he saw his father, and the dogs, the pig and the old woman all singing, his father holding a shovel, the old woman's house crumbled and then raised.

The dog growled. Terry kicked the ground. It looked to be mostly wolf, but its tongue was fat and purple, almost black. He was set in his mind to gut it. He took a step, and the dog clenched, pulled back some in the dark. A streetlamp stuttered yellow on the corner.

I'll cut your ears off.

He waved the shank. The tip caught the dog's eyes. He did it a few times, and then he took his arm down slow and put it on the ground between them. He put his hands up, showed the dog his bare palms. The dog's face went still. They pondered each other this way for a few moments. He leaned some more, turned his hand over and moved it slow beneath the dog's nose, mouth blotted red, breath warm at his skin.

Be quiet now.

He let the dog breathe at his hand and smell it, and then he moved it behind the ears and kneaded the skin.

Get to it then.

He stood up and pointed at the trees behind.

Go on.

For a moment the dog looked at him, and then it turned and made to the woods.

30

THE NEXT day, early, he went back to the sporting goods to get some shoes for his father. In their cardboard box the running shoes bulged his jacket a hump when he tucked them at his belly, sucked back toward his spine and up, into his ribs, fastened the plastic quarter buttons at the front flap. He took the box from his jacket, and then he set it down against the floor. He thought for a moment on what made the best course; he checked the aisle again. He bent down and scooped the shoebox, straightened up then and raised his left arm high at the shoulder, lodged the box long against his ribs, held it there tight when he dropped his arm down to keep it steady and wrapped the coat over.

Terry left the box on the kitchen table. Then he thought to wrap it, but he couldn't find any paper in the house like that, so he got newspaper from the bin, unfolded the big front section and put the box to it, and then he wrapped it over the top, got clear plastic tape and fastened the seams, and then he left it there again, on the small kitchen table, where his father would sit.

The running shoes looked more like socks than shoes, off white with a red stripe on the sides and a red heel tab. That runner on television, the one whose heart worked different than most people, got more air and beat steady when he ran far and fast, he wore shoes like that.

Later Benjamin Webber came home and studied the box and then he took the shoes out and held them at the knot where the laces were tied together. They dangled beneath, a tree ornament, and he looked them over. He undid the laces, sat down and pulled his boots off at the heel. He put one foot, then the other in the running shoes, and then he tied them, stood up and worked his heels and forefeet around inside them. He rocked back and forth some, toe to heel. He walked a lap in the kitchen, and then he stopped beside the small table, looked down at the shoes and rocked some more.

Benjamin Webber said, I want to sleep in them.
Terry said, I think they will make you very fast.

31

SHE GOT him between classes, yanked his knapsack down from behind, pulled his shoulders back. He stopped then, and looked at her, and she didn't speak, but tugged at his sleeve, led him beneath the doorway to a classroom the school used to store desks. They stood shoulder to shoulder, watched kids pass in front of them, moving through the hall before fourth period bell. When they thinned, she leaned out and looked both ways.

Come on, she said.

She looked again, and then she stepped from beneath the arch, held his fingers with hers, led him onto a quiet walk to the hall exit leading behind the school.

They kept their heads down, over to the teachers' lot, pulled hood ornaments from hold slots on three of them, left them cocked, dislodged, drooped one side or the other, and then they crossed the practice field, got close to the trees on the east side. She pointed.

What I wanted you to see, she said.

He looked; an owl, bigger than any he'd seen, even in pictures, knee high if standing it looked to him, laid to its back, eyes long and dark, like a person's, one wing splayed a little, the other tucked behind, wide, fat feet, like a labrador. One foot clutched a headless crow, like a banded newspaper wrapped in plastic, thrown to door stoop. He looked some more, couldn't figure how it was dead, no wounds, no bullet holes or tire marks on the great owl, just dropped there, left to rot beneath long pine. He wanted to touch it, but would not. He figured lightning, but the feathers were untouched. He looked at Alice, scrunched his face a question. She shrugged.

I don't know, she said. Just fell I guess.

Just fell? he said. Don't make sense.

She shrugged again.

Maybe it was just old, she said. Maybe it was just tired.

THEY DROVE early, no cars on the road, got an hour south and passed a lake, and then the capitol, a white dome. Only a few cars, even then. Another thirty miles they stopped for gas, and she showed him the rest of the way; she drew a finger line on the map west, across green and pink and orange states, mountains and rivers and state parks and towns, her hands red from the cold; she blew at them. Floodlights at the station pumps behind them turned off, and the new light sprung. They swore hunched over the flat country unfolded on the hood, the lot of those fuckers, the whole town, even, were forgotten already, so early, its face blurred a drunk fingerprint.

They got back on beneath long clouds, steel gray, and they passed cars gone north on the other side and sometimes they came up on cars in the south lane. Someone had yanked out the back hitch and left a hole in the panel. The metal around it rusted back to a lip. She had covered it with a square patch of cardboard, edges layered shut with duct tape. He watched the metal back door stutter, and then he watched her head through the glass nod. He worked at a joint and passed a long ditch filled up with rainwater. He smoked half and pinched it out and got an empty cigarette box from the floorboard, put the stub in the box and tossed it on the passenger side.

A combine turned a dead cornfield and a wire fence posted shoulder high for two miles, and then a water tower, and then he kept his eyes too long on a tree shaking with cowbirds gone purple and red in the early light and didn't know he let the front end drift until the fender caught the guardrail and kicked sparks; they rained a tail past his window open to trees in the median, and he watched it pass fired and orange, and then the sparks cleared and he righted the car and put his face back to the road. The rust he colored blue flaked at the wind, rushed over the hood. Once more quickly he turned over his shoulder to the tree, the birds become leaves.

He drank some of the gas station coffee and it burned the roof of his mouth and his tongue. He lipped the cup and tuned the radio through fuzz and then he clicked it off. When it was quiet he thought for a while about space, and everything contained in it, planets and chairs and dogs and weather, and he was glad to be awake, and stoned, quickly moving through cold sharp air, and he was glad of the girl he followed, and of the new year, and he was glad of the morning, the blue light plain on the road. The tree and the birds and the sparks from the fender that soon were portents, and for good, signs the world had an energy, just there, like the pitch of fast water, or burning leaves.

Her car started to wobble, but he did not worry. It was old, a gray station wagon with mismatched and balding wheels, wood panel at the sides and back hitch; he figured the alignment was bad. He watched it shake. Four exits passed.

He tried the radio again, and found nothing. He got the box from the passenger seat and went back at the joint and when it burned his lips he rolled down the window and held an arm over the frame and dropped the end. He left the window and screamed at the trees gone by for some miles and his feet wanted to dance like mad, and they swiped the pedals and lurched the car, and the cold air rushed the window and smelled like burnt wood, and he held his mouth closed and pushed air from both nostrils, and it fogged inside the car with the window down, and it fogged inside with the window up and the heat off. He pressed an asthma inhaler and held his breath. He stared long at a billboard. It read WISE MEN SEEK HIM.

Her car turned sideways and rolled onto its head and slid into the median, which was mostly small pine, and long dry grass. He watched this all as if it were a dance.

He slowed his car and pulled onto the shoulder and got out.

Her car rested still upside down and left a path mashed brown back to the interstate. The wheels were still turning. The front right was torn, and it clapped against the metal going around, and the top of the car was pressed flat.

The window glass was smashed out, and the seatbelt was still across her chest and over her lap. Her head touched the roof. Her eyes were closed and her neck bent forward sharply so her chin went down into the collarbone. There was some blood but not so much.

One of the side mirrors was snapped off and laid at his feet and he picked it up. He turned and threw the mirror at the road.

He leaned at the driver's side and put his hands flat on some of her hair run over the frame.

A truck pulled in behind him. Then an old man stood beside in the gray light and asked about the turned car. Terry pressed on her hair, turned his head to the old man. He opened his mouth to speak and then he stopped. The words slipped, weren't there to begin with. He went back to his hands and looked.

There was a police car and an ambulance. The policeman made him take his hands off her hair. There was some glass beneath but he didn't feel it. The policeman said his hands were bleeding.

One of the ambulance drivers quickly taped his hands, and then two of them zipped her up and lifted her into the back. One of them shut the doors. One said she was busted something unnatural. One touched his right shoulder and kept a hand there.

He sat in the grass on the shoulder and watched her move away in white and orange lights. He was not yet a man. He wanted a bomb to go off and light the gray sky. The police car waited on him to stand. He didn't pull the glass out of his hands, not for a long time.

H E ASKED to drive. The policeman wore a gray uniform and a wide round hat with dents in the top and he shook his head and told him it wouldn't work because of his hands cut to shit and then he called a tow on the radio and they left the car on the interstate and the keys in the front seat.

He picked one edge of the tape at his hands until the gauze peeled back. The skin was gummed. He balled the tape with the gauze and dabbed the cuts for a few minutes and then he dropped the ball to the floorboard. Some of the cuts went to bleeding again, and he poked at them with a finger to see if there was glass still, and then he pressed his hands against his thighs for a few minutes until they stopped.

Soon they passed the crest of the bridge, and the old downtown surfaced below them; behind and in front of the car, lamps raised on joints in the bridge dropped in measured white. He knocked the safety plastic between the front and back and put his head close and the plastic was scratched and cloudy. The policeman kept his head straight and reached behind and slid open a small door in the center of the guard panel.

I don't have any money, Terry said.

The policeman put a forearm on the seat ledge. He turned over his shoulder and then back to the road, but kept an ear to the door. He had a faded tattoo on his forearm, dark blue line, a navy anchor, and a pinup with bobbed hair standing on top, hips cocked, the word Enola above that.

Say again, he said.

For the tow. I can't pay.

It's nothing. It's a friend of mine pulling it.

He thought to tell the policeman to leave it for the rust and the weather but he'd taped a paper bag with some strong dope wrapped up in plastic beneath the passenger seat. He leaned back against the blue vinyl, wanted to ask about the tattoo and where that word came from. The policeman turned again, and Terry poked at the cuts on one hand and then he poked at the other ones.

You and that girl were going off.

Yeah.

Terry rubbed the left wrist with his right hand and did the other one the same.

You're not old enough.

Terry shook his head.

Yeah, he said.

He rubbed his wrists some more.

You see what happens?

Yeah.

The tow beat them. The car sat in the driveway facing the house. The policeman stayed in his car and Terry got out and came around the trunk and the policeman waved him at the driver's side. His other forearm was on the sill, a scuffed gold watch at the wrist and another tattoo above the watch, cowboy pistol with the hammer pulled back. It was blue lined, dark and faded, like the other. He took the arm away and leaned to the passenger seat, raised back straight and held a folded knife through the frame. Terry looked at him, and then he looked at the knife.

Take it.

It was heavy, lock blade, a wooden handle with brass at both ends, deep blood groove on the blade.

I'm not supposed to give knives out. Keep it low now.

Terry put the knife in his front shirt pocket. It pulled down the cloth inside.

I won't say anything, he said.

We pick up lots of things from people. I mean I got a trunk full. Clubs and chains and spikes.

Terry nodded, fingered the handle at his chest.

You know how to use it?

He took the knife from his shirt, turned it over and studied it. He unfolded the blade and held it straight up, waved it and got lost in the point back and forth in the light. He pointed the blade at the policeman and pushed it toward him. The policeman looked down slow at the knife and then he looked at the boy and cocked his head some at one side.

Turn it around, he said.

Terry turned the knife handle first. The policeman took it at the wood grip, folded it shut, looked hard at Terry for a few moments, not speaking. He nodded quick and held the knife to him.

Terry watched the car grow small on the road, beneath yellow lamplight. He stood at the front door. The house was locked, empty, everything same as the morning. What he thought was, this is my lot. His father was still at work. He pulled shut the front door of the house and turned the deadbolt from the outside.

Later he opened the passenger side and leaned on the floorboard with the knife. He went beneath the seat and cut the electric tape holding the paper bag to the bottom. He shut the door and went to the other side. He pulled the seatbelt over his chest. He thought to leave, finish what they'd started, back from the driveway and make west, and he cranked the car and let it idle and clenched his left hand at the drive stick a few times. He smoked some of the dope with a metal pipe and it heated and burned his lips. He listened to cars on the street behind him.

HE RAN hot water and a bar of soap through the work gloves and dried them in the oven, wore them on his hands while he slept, and in the morning his father didn't wake him, and he didn't wake him the day after, and Terry slept to late afternoon and woke dry mouthed, body sore. The back of his thighs ached, in the center, down to the knee bend, and a muscle running from his left shoulder up his neck to his head felt twisted and wound tight. The fabric stuck at the cuts leaked in the night and he pulled them off in the kitchen, wrung the gloves with water and soap again and set them to dry on the counter, and then he washed his hands with dish soap, and no blood then, but the cut lines were puffed and raw. He made fists. Light broke trees in the backyard, the pine twitched. He heard the front door shut hard in the frame.

His father found him smoking on the back steps. He held the door for him to come back inside. He sat near the middle of the couch, and Terry sat on the chair facing him, both hunched over their knees.

You still tired?

Terry nodded, and rubbed a spot on the back of his neck.

You sore?

My neck hurts some.

You need to get some ice.

Alright.

Benjamin Webber looked at him, and then he turned his face down to the space between his thighs. He stayed that way and pushed on the backs of his hands with his thumbs.

You can't run away again.

Terry nodded.

They'll take you off.

I won't do it anymore.

You don't want to come with me. I know that. There's no choice here though. You understand that?

TWO DAYS he stayed in his room and kept the door locked. His father knocked hard a few times. Terry didn't say anything. Clouds through his window were low and gray, full of a storm to the south. He thought of her as a dark shot of birds over a field, a spray of black wings and chatter, all one thing, beating with many hearts. His father knocked again.

Listen.

Go away, Terry said.

His head rocked. He couldn't sort anything out, not her gone to ash, or the man past the door.

I need you to be away from that door.

You can say whatever you want, his father said.

Leave me the hell alone.

If talking to someone is what you need.

I fucking hear you, now leave.

He didn't mean for it that way, but the words came a scream. His face jerked a sob; it clenched, hard, and he felt each of his teeth at once when he bit down. He put a hand over his eyes and turned to his lap. He took the policeman knife from his pocket and threw it closed against the door. It broke a notch shoulder high, chipped the floor when it fell. His father put a fist hard on the wood. The thud jerked him. The room was quiet, and then his father struck the door harder, and then three times quickly, with more weight. Terry went back to the dark clouds through his window.

You got nothing to say to me.

There was a pause, and then the hardest knock yet. Terry's face slacked. He breathed slow, waited for footsteps backed away.

He tried to cry afterwards, but nothing came, and he stayed in his room smoking dope. He burnt candles until the wick lilted and they melted on his dresser. He put the tips of his fingers into the wax, and it didn't hurt so much. He took the knife from the floor and unfolded it and cut slits on top of his knuckles. He kneeled at the floor vent, and put his face close; the air came through cold. He shut his eyes and spoke into the vent.

Tell me where I am, he said.

THEY BURNED her very hotly, and then she was ash and wind. He didn't sleep at night. He went to school at seven-thirty and slept in class. He slept through a knifing in the gymnasium, and then he slept through most of what the principal called a riot; in the courtyard, on lunch hour, kids from all four grades set flame to trash and textbooks in the metal bins, and then they lit cans in the halls. He woke up in detention when he heard the shrill firebell, the teacher beside him, rocking his shoulder, forearm at her mouth, eyes watered. He coughed, stood up and followed the rest of them outside, smoke from the windows and doors, low over the buildings like a factory burn.

THE MENTHOL display next to the register in the gas station had all kinds, light and regular and ultralight and short and long. He dropped a handful of five-cent pink chewing gum at the counter. The old man went slow counting the pieces. Terry got two packs at his beltline. He went back the next afternoon. After four days he had ten packs, six days he had twenty.

Curtis Rigby came over to buy some. Terry stood at a small fire he built in the backyard. He tossed one shoe. It caught, the canvas bent the fire blue, and he let it go a few minutes. Curtis stood beside him. Terry got a stick and poked the shoe in the fire. He scratched the back of his head. He scratched it some more.

Something is wrong with you, Curtis said.

Probably.

He tossed the other shoe.

It's good luck dammit, Terry said.

Who told you that?

I can't remember.

My legs hurt. They're sore.

Must have run somewhere in your dream.

Can I get those smokes, man?

Terry took the stick from the fire and pointed it at the porch, the tip coal orange.

Up there, he said.

Curtis went up to the porch and rustled the paper bag. He came back to the fire, carried one pack at his armpit, thumped another against his forearm.

How old are you? Terry said.

Fourteen dammit. Same as you.

I'm fifteen.

Oh.

Curtis gave him two dollars. He charged double on the risk. Curtis started off from the yard, and Terry watched him leave. He scratched his head some more, and then he went up on the porch and got another pack of cigarettes. He went fast down the steps and yelled at him in the road. Curtis turned around and started to come back.

That's all the money I've got man, he said.

Terry held the pack to him, and then he went to his pockets and gave him back the two dollars. Curtis looked at him confused, and then he said thank you, and Terry nodded at him, and didn't speak, and then he left Curtis in the road and went back to the yard and the fire.

Terry cut a deep gash on his index finger messing with the knife. He pressed the finger hard against his thigh for a few minutes to cap the blood but it wouldn't stop. He pressed the finger some more and still the cut stayed open. He cut the sleeve from an old shirt and then he cut a strip from that and wrapped it tight around the cut. He was out of cigarettes. He went up to the filling station. It was almost eleven at night. The night clerk was there. He didn't see her much. He pointed at the cigarettes in the rack behind her and she turned around and got them and then she put them on the counter. Terry held over a dollar. She rang the cash drawer open. She put the change in his hand and looked at the cloth bandaged on his finger.

What's wrong with your finger? she said.

Nothing's wrong with my finger, he said.

You got that wrap on the end of it. It's all bloody.

A shark bit it, alright?

When?

When I was in the ocean.

Oh.

When I was swimming around in the ocean.

Was it a big shark?

I tried to poke it in the eyes with my thumbs. I saw that on television.

But it bit you on the finger.

Yes.

You're brave.

I know.

He got his cigarettes and left the store.

38

THE GIRL sitting ahead of him came in mornings smelling woodstove and destitute. Terry's head itched, and he scratched at it with his tooth-bit fingernails. The civics teacher, a man shaped like an apple, called Charles Hawthy, stopped talking and asked him to come up front. Terry raised from his desk, up front stood with his back to the class, at one side of the teacher's metal desk. Terry smelled the aftershave he used, the kind on television with the pearl white bottle and the pirate ship on front, and felt his stomach turn when he did. He hated the smell; it made him think of the rich man, Nola Walker, and others like him, handshakes and white tooth smiles, church clothes and money clips. Charles Hawthy looked close at his hair and shook his head.

Leave now, he said. Go straight to the nurse.

Terry didn't understand. The girl in front of his desk wrote at her paper. Charles Hawthy got him by the arm and tugged him at the door.

All of us will end up with it, all of us, he said. Can you be responsible for that? Can you?

He pushed Terry into the hall and shut the door hard. Terry scratched one side of his head, and then the other one, and then the top and the back.

The nurse found lice. She wore plastic gloves and picked at his hair.

How did you get this? she said.

I don't know, Terry said.

Do you wash your hair?

Sometimes.

How much?

Sometimes.

She went to a cabinet and got a small white bottle and gave it to him. He looked it over.

Use it twice today, twice tomorrow, then you need to wash your hair every day, soap, hot water, it doesn't matter.

Terry nodded and put the bottle in the inside pocket of his jacket.

They start to come back, you see me alright?

Thank you, he said.

He walked past the door to his class, and he kept going, and then he pushed the double doors near the front offices and made down the main walk. No one came after. He walked on the shoulder.

ERRY TRADED the hatchback even for an eleven-year-old Monte Carlo with tee tops. The engine was eight cylinder, and the paint job something for a bowling ball, shiny and metal green. The roof section was black cloth, and torn in a few places. He pressed the brakes long before he wanted to stop; through a rusted hole in the floorboard he watched the road pass beneath. He didn't take the windows off to let the roof open, but he thought of it; the idea of a roof with windows he could take out and put in the trunk made him dizzy it felt so unnecessary and glamorous. The windows came with padded storage sleeves, dark green vinyl, like the inside of the car, heavy brass zipper on top to hold them safe.

Terry woke standing, naked in the fore room, except for the red band work socks sagged at his ankles. He was going at a piss; for how long he was not sure; he dreamt of rain, and the sound of his piss against the wood panel sounded like rain pelting the roof, and he thought, still, it was rain, when he looked down at himself, head still half in dream, and he watched the piss for a few moments, thought, at the same time, it is raining, and too, I'm going on the wall.

He held the piss and ran outside, socks damp in the early dewed grass, stood on pine straw bedded thick around an oak, and he went there, back to piss, first on the bark and then at the root-knobbed base of the tree. He kept going when it started to rain. He looked up, heard winter thunder above him, past the branches.

40

H E MEANT to scout the place. He watched television, so he knew thieves and robbers and that kind, people who did things like burgle houses, they cased joints before a break-in, studied people for the comings and goings, did it a week, sometimes a month. He drove his car early, on a Monday, a few blocks over, locked the doors and walked a path through the woods. He crouched near the treeline behind her house, smoked cigarettes, part of a joint. He admired the rose garden in back. He put a hand through his hair. It was soft from the lice shampoo the nurse gave to him, smelled of strawberries and chlorine. He scratched above his right ear. His head itched less. He watched her parents leave close to eight; first the father, then the mother. She was an inventor, owned a restaurant supply store full of clear plastic beverage pitchers. She conjured one with two wide pouring spouts on the sides, plus the one on front, and her patent wouldn't expire for many years. Her father worked there, for her mother.

Late afternoon he woke in the same spot. He rubbed his eyes, and then he checked the sun for the time. The mother came home after four. She parked the car in the yard and got out, had a cigarette in her mouth, white, long and skinny. She was tall, wore a knee-length black skirt, and she walked the drive and pulled the smoke a few times, twisted the end at grass lining the walk. She checked to see if the tip still burned, put the stub in a shirt pocket, and then she stuck the key to the brass deadbolt above the doorknob.

The father pulled in an hour later. He was round and short, had dark slicked hair, wore a powder blue oxford, tan slacks with severe pleats. There was a sticker at both sides of the bumper on his four-door burgundy sedan. One read, RIDE A BIKE TODAY! The other, TAKE A HIKE!

Terry watched the house quiet until dark and cut grooves at his left knuckles with the police knife. He pressed hard to break the skin.

Next morning he went back, worked again at his knuckles with the knife and watched Alice's parents turn their cars, exhaust from the tails like great storms in the early weak light. He watched them back down the drive, same as the morning before. He waited a half hour, folded the knife and stuck it to his sock pulled high above the bootlip. He wrapped his hand in part of his shirt and held it tight at the cuts, and then he squeezed a fist and waited for blood that did not come back.

The house smelled clean and quiet, like fruit, or snow. In the main room he stood at the mantel and stared on the pictures; one of Alice a baby, one of her sister Nora in Colorado. She stood on a great field, the whole of the world behind, bright and blue and absent of cloud. She held her arms high. Terry picked up the frame, turned it over. It was silver, glass at the front. He looked at the wood floor. He dropped the picture, and then he bent down and gathered it up. The glass cracked. He got a few pieces on the floor, tossed them at the ashes in the fireplace and covered them over, and then he put the silver frame in the fire and covered it too. He folded the picture and stuck it to his back pocket, looked again at the one of Alice on the mantel, turned it facedown.

He opened closet doors in the hall and looked inside at their brooms and winter coats. He stood at the open doorway of her parents' room at the end of the hall and crossed his arms over his chest. He lit a cigarette, went inside and sat down on the bed, knocked ashes in the pillows, and then he went to the bathroom and put the cigarette in the toilet.

Alice's room was next to her parents'. The walls were bare. He opened drawers at the water-stained dresser; towels, sheets. In the bottom right there were a few of her things; Virgin Mary night light, old black camera, cassette tapes, a picture of her and her sister and mother and father in front of a Christmas tree with white lights, yellow coffee cup filled with pennies. He closed the drawer and sat down on her bed. He pressed one hand into the mattress, got the picture from his back pocket and held it up and read the back and looked on front at her sister in the field. He lay down on the bed and looked up at the ceiling and let the picture sit flat on his chest. The fan moved slow and dizzy. He pulled the pale blue cover at one side of the bed over his shoulders, put his face into it and breathed hard through his nose. He meant to smell her, but nothing, and then he was asleep.

Her mother stood above him and smoked a cigarette, one arm crossed a slant on her chest and tucked beneath the other one. She held the cigarette high, near her face, blew smoke in the room. He blinked hard a few times to make sure. She knocked ashes to a hand.

Did you think I wouldn't know you were here? she said.

He thought a moment. No words came. He pushed the spread back and sat up. She moved easy through the room, got a small wood chair at one corner, drug it over and sat down. She tapped ashes at her hand again and closed a fist. She wore the silver hoop earrings Alice used to pierce her ear. He thought to pull one out, and laid one hand over the other in his lap. She put the cigarette in her mouth, and leaned toward him, took his hands and turned them over and put her thumbs on the cuts. He studied her eyes, pinched in the smoke, took his hands from her and jammed them beneath his arms. He got up off the bed and straightened the pillow and then the spread. He turned back to her; if he didn't ask, he never would, the question in his head a gleaming bone. They burned her to ash, but past that fact he didn't know what, and it confused him, thought and blood and heart turned to that.

What did you do with her? he said.

Her mother was quiet.

Is there a jar? he said.

She stood up, went over to one wall and opened the window. She took long, quick pulls. He put his eyes to the floor, then lifted his face. She kept hers at the window. She finished the smoke, thumped it to the backyard and then she lit another.

Is she on the mantel? he said.

She kept her face at the backyard and pulled on the smoke and blew from her nose.

Is she in a jar? he said.

She turned quickly, and glared at him.

In a trunk with a combination?

She didn't speak, kept her face at his.

What?

She shook her head.

Is something wrong with you? she said.

I need you to tell me.

She looked away.

No one talks like that, she said.

She kept at the window and her cigarette, a quick hard drag and then another, ash tapped to the sill.

He went on a run and did not think to stop. The trees rushed past were dead or sleeping.

41

TERRY WENT back to Alice's house, three hours before first light. He parked his car in the same place and carried a shovel and a sack of potatoes into her backyard. He started digging at the edge of the rose garden, worked a deep rut beneath the grass and roots. He knifed the sack in the middle and held it to the mouth of the hole and shook it empty. He covered the scar neatly with loose dirt and pine straw from the flowerbed. He dropped the empty potato sack in the field on the way back to the car. He put the shovel in the back and drove off. In two weeks, the rose garden would be dead. Alice's parents would have many potatoes.

42

BENJAMIN WEBBER came outside wearing army boots with black laces undone, tongues loose and flapped at blue church socks pulled close to his knees, legs bare above the bands. They were old shoes, from Korea when he carried a gun there and shot communists from the northern part. Once Benjamin Webber said he used a flamethrower there, and burned a whole forest, and some people inside. The flamethrower took two people to carry, he said, him at the barrel and trigger, metal harness bracing both shoulders to keep the gun still, another at the back, toting the fire tank, both of them zipped burnproof coats and pants and hoods, like a spacesuit he said, or one for scuba diving. He had on flannel sleep pants cut short with scissors, bottoms frayed loose red and black string. The silver hair left on the sides of his head stuck wild from his night face against the pillow. He smoothed it some, but it stayed.

Terry was leaned at one knee beside a fire; leaves and sticks from the yard, low wet plume of smoke wound a bed spring. He pulled up hunks of grass and threw them in. He stood up when he saw his father, and thumbed the cigarette into the dark past. He spit, wiped one corner of his mouth on the back of his green jacket sleeve. He looked for the cigarette after, to see if the cherry still burnt, but nothing, only his father's chest and face streaked with fire line the closer he got; all of him clear when he stood beside Terry and crossed his arms tight on his chest. The end of his nose, the bridge, flushed apple red, broken veins at the nostrils and cheeks, skin beneath his eyes puffed so much Terry couldn't see the bottom lids. Benjamin Webber took a red bandanna from a pocket and put it to his nose and blew hard and high and then he did it again. He folded the cloth and went to put it back but he stopped and held it out. Terry put a hand out and shook his head.

I'm alright, he said. You can keep it.

Benjamin Webber nodded, did not speak, put the kerchief to the pocket on his sleep pants.

Are you related to the ones that invented the grills? I mean us, are we? I've used one before. They're nice.

Maybe it was your great grandfather.

Nah.

A second cousin.

Nope.

I wish it was.

Benjamin Webber did a quick nod.

I do, too, he said.

I bet they get free charcoal. Hot dogs. Marshmallows and all that.

I had a grill one time.

Did you fight Russians?

No. Koreans.

Why does that president always talk about wars with Russians?

He's got a small pecker.

Oh.

Did you really have a blowtorch?

Yeah.

Why?

I burnt things. Houses. People. Trees.

Was your blowtorch cool to use?

No. Nothing like that is cool to use, boy.

His father was convinced he should be on the soccer team. He stood there, scratched skin at his bare thighs flicked orange light, and asked Terry questions; how he felt, good or bad, sad or angry or whatever.

The night after he made a phone call, promised the coach in Echota a box of new school-colored sweatshirts, hooded or straight collared, if Terry could be on the team. The coach said, sure, fine; the team needed sweatshirts, sometimes they got cold.

43

ENJAMIN WEBBER rented a silver family van, boomerang antennae on top, wood panel at the sides. At the rental office, he pulled the two seats shaped like small pews from the back and left them there, cleared box space, and then at the house he stacked their things inside, cardboard flaps sealed with clear postal tape, and labeled with red pen marker. There wasn't room for Terry inside the van. Benjamin Webber gave him five dollars for gas, to drive himself and a few other boxes he couldn't fit into the van. He left a gift on the kitchen block table, a plastic radio with an antenna and a tape player on the front. He took it from the break room at Hardwick after it sat for two weeks with no claim. His own father, July Webber, brought things home from the landfill where he worked; a Belgian made sixteen gauge pump action shotgun, shell pin pulled so the chamber carried five shots instead of three; headboard from a dark finished poster frame bed; phonograph missing needle arm; box kite made from dowel rods, yellow wind cloth the outside skin; brass latched specimen box, shaped like a small briefcase, grasshopper and locust needle pinned to the wood inside, genus and phyla writ card labels beneath; iron woodstove, hole torn at the creosote resined flu pipe; garden spade; gray stone cast of the Buddha; mannequin torso; dark union field coat from the states' war, thick navy wool, gold buttons big as light bulbs, crossed rifles graved at them; iron fireplace grate; pine box nailed shut, tulip bulbs laid to wood shavings inside; none of these remained.

Come on when you get ready, Benjamin Webber said.

Terry nodded, put the bill to his shirt pocket. The radio had a handle on top, like a lunch pail. Terry picked it up from the table and held it in front and studied it.

He sat in the driveway for an hour and played a tape in the radio. Sometimes he looked at the house.

Terry got on the interstate near dark, after five miles there unhitched the knife and thought of the policeman holding it to him, and then he felt hungry, put a hand flat against his belly and held it there. Curtis Rigby said his cousins, ones on his mother's side, they killed wild forest pigs with knives like that, cornered them a circle in the row pine, the sawbrier and bracken, deepstuck the blade to a big artery in the right shoulder flank; with this the boar fell down, and died; then the tick dogs lapped blood. These pigs had mohawks on their heads and on their backs, Curtis Rigby said, tusks, white as piano keys, from the sides of their mouths that diced calves and shins and knees to ribbon shred; they weighed five hundred pounds, sometimes more; they were not scared of people, guns or dogs. Terry never thought of a pig that way; there was a pink one in a book that talked with a spider webbed to a barn rafter; later the pig became the father of its babies after the spider was dead; afterward the pig cried often. Terry thought about a woman's stomach with a baby inside it stretched a drum skin, and then he thought of breakfast, cereal and red jelly sandwiches; he touched his belly, again, remembered, in the park downtown Issaqueena, watching a young, steep-haired woman sitting at a lawn chair, coarse green leaves from the box elders shingled near her feet; Terry heard a baby cry, then another; wet spots formed at her shirt front. She looked down, covered flat palms at her breasts, pulled her jacket tight over her chest and held it closed; when he told Curtis Rigby the next day, standing toe curbed, waiting after last bell for a ride, he got hungry, again, and then he wondered if he always would when the woman from the park reared in his head; Curtis Rigby pulled a book from his knapsack, the one they used in biology, turned it to the index and scrolled his index finger at a column; here, he said; he stopped near the front, past the appendices and periodic table, past the color pictures of rock and mineral, leaned over close at a diagram; the insides of a man and woman, line drawn, organs labeled at the white margin space. He mumbled the words while he read the paragraph beneath, told Terry a woman, like many other mammals, could lactate, spontaneously, upon hearing a baby cry; says it right here, he said; Terry told him he didn't understand, and Curtis Rigby said, Look, it's simple, you know how you smell, like, something that smells like weed, or somebody else smoking weed, and then you want to smoke it? Terry nodded. Same thing, Curtis Rigby said.

Terry held the knife blade up the whole way, fingers tight on the wood-grained handle, butt end resting on the dash. He looked for wild pigs on the side of the road, heads poked from the trees, mean black hair, grinning bull horn.

44

TERRY STARTED school in Echota the day after. It rained full on the way, trees bent to cold water. The green river beneath a small concrete bridge ran high at the pilings and foamed a sheet over the road. His tires gave some, wobbled through the slick. The radio shook in the seat, and the bridge ended, the ground looked up and the tires bit the road hard, town behind a smear of railroad and tin.

He listened to a record called *Combat Rock* by a group named the Clash. He'd taped it to a cassette, played it then in the plastic radio he'd set on the passenger seat. The radio was metal gray, the size of a breadbox, a fold-out handle on top. He faced the black web speakers at the windshield, believed the slant of glass pushed the music from the speakers over his head, against the ceiling and to the back of the car and the rear glass, and there it bent down, over the backseat, along the floor, under the front seat to his shoes and the pedals, kept that way, moved the way heat filled a room. Alice Washington told him all about Joe Strummer. He thought of him, then, his job cleaning toilets at the English National Opera before the Clash got started, climbing rafters sixty feet with a wire cutter longway in his mouth like a horse bit to steal a microphone. Terry wanted to love something that way. All the headlights he passed in the wet morning were suns burning out. An early joint put everything to a moan; he knew later, at soccer practice, he'd get pummeled.

The Echota school was square and dark brick on the outside. Exhaust fans shaped like globes turned on the flat roof, and steam came out and fissured just above the metal. The main yard edged short trees and a concrete walk. The cars of teachers nudged the curb. Two sides were shallow fields, the ruin of pine between the school and highway. He put the asthma inhaler to his mouth and pulled hard and held it in. He'd gotten it from the school nurse. She gave it to him after he went in and said his throat was tight and he couldn't breathe so good. She'd listened to his chest with a stethoscope.

Inside he was led by color; the white and black check of the cafeteria floor just past the front glass, the pale yellow and blue walls, the wood brown railing of staircase rising to the second floor. He blazed the halls for a smoking section, and found none, and then he went to the front office where the principal and all those other bastards lived. It was quiet inside, no one behind the counter. Terry leaned to it, put his knees against the flat panel below the counter, fished out his pack of cigarettes and held them. He waited a few minutes, knuckled the veneer with a four-count tap, he rang a tin bell; one like a hotel must have, he thought, a chime for a bellman.

A teacher came from the back offices and faced him. Terry showed him the cigarettes, held the new pack out over the counter. The teacher wore a wine rouge blazer, pale carnation pinned to the lapel. He looked down, bone white hair long at the neck, then swept thin wisps over the crown, and lingered at Terry's hand, the smokes gripped there, amber tint bifocals low on the bridge of his nose. Terry looked at the pack, too, then back up, quickly; the teacher's wet yellow boutonniere and his staring confused him.

What? Terry said. Stop looking at my hand.

The teacher reached over and took the pack; Terry lurched to get them back.

Hey, he said.

The teacher yanked the cigarettes past his reach, held them up and broke the pack in the middle. He took a few steps and dropped them past one end of the counter to a trash bin on the floor below.

Hey, man. Hey. You owe me a dollar for those.

I don't.

Can I have the busted ones back? What do you say?

No.

I was looking for the smoking section.

You can't smoke here.

What?

The school board says it.

What does that mean?

They don't allow it.

They did at my old school.

This isn't your old school. Be quiet.

Can I have that dollar?

Two times you get caught, the teacher told him, it's school on Saturday, eight hours bagging trash, painting classroom trailer walls. Then he dropped his eyes to the counter and opened a thick ring binder and flipped through. He stopped past the middle pages and kept his face there a moment, and then he closed the book, and set it back. He got a pen and wrote on an index card, and then he came back and stood at the counter and faced him. Terry shifted his weight, pad to heel.

Please can I have those cigarettes, man?

The teacher put the white card on the counter and tapped it with his left index finger.

Your schedule, he said.

He raised an arm and pointed over Terry's right shoulder, through the glass-laced break wire.

End of this hall is your class, he said.

Terry stopped at a tan cinder block bathroom. He pushed the metal slide lock in the stall, and put his back against the door. He dug at the big zip pocket on front of his knapsack and found an old pack with three left. He put it to his mouth and blew, rounded the soft pack with his breath and shook one out. He struck a match, pulled through his mouth and blew smoke from his nose. He waved his hands to break the cloud. The cherry burned long, orange and pointed. The filter turned in on itself. The speed and volume of things grew sudden then, and the world moved quick, jagged, sped then slowed by a hand he could not figure; he saw dot-nosed warheads, butted through doors in the great plains, Alice Washington held seatbelt to her chest, upside down in her crushed car; he heard wedding music. The sound outside grew, and thumped, so loud he let go of the rail and put his hands to his ears; whetstone, a hungry ghost, music never listened to, stuck past his hands beneath the hair and bone. His eyes rolled, back pressed hard on the door; bells rang high on the hall brick, heels from the classrooms grew loud on the tile, he went to dream.

A fist against the locked door at his back and his head shook straight. His lips tasted singed plastic. He took his hands from his ears and let the smoke drop from his mouth to the toilet water. The fist knocked again.

I heard goddammit, he said.

He pushed through the door and shouldered a tall kid with stringy black hair, said what he thought was, I'm a visitor.

During classes he sat in back of the room and kept his eyes down. The teachers called his name.

In the hall shoulders knocked him down twice. Both times he stood quiet and kept walking.

At the last bell he went fast to the front doors and lit a smoke in the yard. He threw it down next to his car, opened the door and got inside, pressed a button on top of the radio to play the tape.

He turned left and drove the long cracked highway run in front of the school. The houses shrank, split to field, air warm and red at the window, a lull, like first light. He pulled a joint stub from the ashtray. He parked in the concrete lot beside the practice field, and leaned to the backseat. He sifted trash in the floorboard for shin guards and socks zipped in a blue and red duffel bag from his father's closet.

The sport was new in the state. They played it in Russia, Terry thought, and Europe, Germany, east and west, and Mexico, and the country vampires came from, Transylvania. In Issaqueena there were two teams for Pickens County, green and blue, and Terry played green, for Stay Loaded Dump Trucks of West Issaqueena. Blue was sponsored by Issaqueena

Pawn and Gun. Dixon Brown's father was the coach. He stood them in two rows. They lost all five games in the season; end of the last one he made everyone charge the other goal. Dixon Brown flattened a kid to a sheet of water. It was November. They stood over him, and breathed smoke. The kid clutched one hand at the busted leg, and the other flailed on the ground, the bone through the shin a sharp white key. The kid screamed. Terry thought of fireworks, and red popsicles.

Terry could kick, but not much past. He didn't have the head for seeing far into the game. He couldn't conjure how things might shape on one end of the grass while play was at the other. He thought there was a fury in him, but he didn't have the body to dole it. He was not swift.

A group of players sat on the shoulder of the field closest to his car, and a few were on the far side and ran the chalk line, the kicked dirt and broken grass, clouds at their feet.

He sat one end of the row and faced the field. The coach came from behind them. For a few minutes he spoke on teamwork, and patience, and the stone necessity of drills. He smoked three cigarettes while he paced a short line in front of them. He dropped them, and they kept smoking in the grass. Terry liked people who smoked. The kids on the team wore old softball league shirts with sponsor names like Pointed Lumber or Haven Florist pasted on front, block numbers at the back; most wore cleats ground to nubs. Terry's cleats were the same, one size too big, quarter holes on the heels. He wore a mail order gray sweatshirt with a picture of a cat from a popular comic strip printed on the front. The cat was orange, boggle eyed, and lived in the nation's capital, near the white dome where the actor president lived and slicked his coal black hair. The cat was fond of snorting at a pile of cocaine, and liked to pal around with a penguin that was very short and responsible. The penguin wore a top hat, and carried a cane, and sometimes he thought to find a friend like that penguin; clear eyes, steady hands. The coach was small, and he wore a thick dark beard. The school's mascot was a bear who smiled with big square teeth, and wore a navy and white beanie. The bear's face was stitched into the front pocket of the coach's white shirt. He cocked his head to the ones running, the front three near the southwest corner of the practice field.

Just because you don't get into some game and run around yelling and spitting like bulldogs.

The runners passed at his back. The coach didn't turn, but kept his face to the players sat in front of him. He sauntered, light folded around his head.

Unless all of you are here, and want to be, do your damn best, or we can't move.

Terry thought him a lover of animals; wished to ask if it were true.

The coach split them into pairs. He pointed at Terry, and then he pointed to a dirty looking kid on his left. The players spread out to the field and kept a distance from each other. He followed the dirty looking one to a spot near the middle of the west end.

You're new.

Looks that way.

Terry didn't know what else to say. The kid's hair was almost orange, long and thin, hairline a bent elbow. His face was patched red, head too big for his hunched shoulders.

How long you been here?

A few days.

You got a car?

Yeah.

I just got one. It's got a good engine.

When the ball got close Terry put one cleat on top, held, and kicked it back.

What's yours like? the dirty kid said.

My car?

The engine.

I think it's good. There's an eight cylinder.

Bullshit.

Yeah.

Sonofabitch. That's a fucking tiger, man.

Alright.

A good engine's important.

Terry thought this might be true, but he wasn't sure.

Does it drive good?

I think so.

What does the speedometer go to?

He hadn't looked enough times to remember, and didn't like so many questions about cars, either. To get an answer, he thought of other cars, numbers buried in their dashes; the blue hatchback; Alice Washington's gray station wagon; police cars; an ambulance. He thought to say eighty, but it seemed low.

A hundred I think.

Mine goes up to one forty. That's just what the numbers say, I mean. It's probably more like one sixty. My dad told me he flipped it back to zero.

What?

All the way around, like past one eighty.

The dirty kid stopped talking, and they kicked the ball between them in slow straight lines.

After drills there was scrimmage. The field was marked holes, grass trod a patchwork. Terry's head had not yet cleared; the coach put him at defender with the second team. He stood around and waited for things to happen, dumb and stoned, loud voices on the field; a forward ran through him full speed and knocked him flat on the dirt; the air got colder.

The goalkeeper, tall, with what looked white hair, reminded Terry of a scarecrow, and kept screaming at him.

Fucking play, he said.

Terry glared at him, straight and hard, and shook a hand that way.

I hear you jackass.

The second time someone knocked him over, the force of the tackle stretched his ribs and yanked his head back. Terry felt lifted from the earth; flyblown, and tossed down. On the grass he couldn't remember a moment between his words with the goalkeeper and someone planting a shoulder to his back; coach yelled for him to get off the field and sit. His knee was bleeding, dirt on his face.

The dirty kid was sat down, too, eyes pinched. He scowled and seemed to ponder something difficult, kept his head straight a moment, then looked down. He pulled up a small twist of grass and put it to his mouth, crammed it with two fingers at one cheek, closed his mouth and chewed slow, a cow gnashing new cud.

Where did you get that beard, anyway?

Terry put a hand to his chin and then both cheeks. It didn't feel much like a beard, gaps on his jaw and at the sides, whiskers poked straight, steel wool. One morning he left for school and his father said there's a cat I know that will lick that dirt off your face if you put some milk on it; he stayed at his newspaper and laughed but did not look up.

There's not much of a beard, Terry said.

It is. You should be happy. I had a Cherokee for a grandmother. I'll never get one, not like that.

Terry didn't understand. He stayed quiet.

They pulled the hair out of their faces for some reason. Cherokees did.

What's that grass taste like?

Grass.

He had a pinch left in one hand, and held it to Terry.

You can have it if you want.

Terry looked at the same grass beneath his knees and everywhere else.

I'll get some later maybe.

The dirty kid threw down the ends.

It's for my stomach anyway, not the taste. It helps with digestion, the fiber.

He spit the mouthful and winced, pulled another bunch and jabbed it the same cheek.

I learned it from a dog, he said.

The dirty kid snorted, hawked deep at his throat and spit.

45

TERRY STOOD by the drink machines at lunch the next day, and the next after that, and two weeks after that; pictures on the drink machines lit from inside, large sweating red aluminum cans waist deep in ice. He thought a few times to unplug one of the drink machines, but couldn't figure what good something like that could do other than hold warm drinks it wouldn't even give out because it was dead with no electricity.

When his name was called he raised a hand. A few times he said present, or here.

In the halls after bells there were knapsacks, forest green, navy blue and black and gray, dull red, a rare orange or yellow, all moving toward lockers and other rooms and each other, and he was at front and at back and inside and everywhere at once within these stacked bags.

Every so often these mountains burst open and cleared a hole in the center and someone got beat into bone meal. He saw two fights up close. The first left one kid holding a clump of red hair. In the other a short, pale girl, hair and eyeliner the same boot black, took a cheap hit from over her shoulder, but quickly she shook her head right, got the one who suckered her by the shirt front and tackled her hard against the block wall. The girl's head made a dull sound when it slammed back and she fell down.

46

AT PRACTICE he ran fast and kicked; during these weeks thought of maps, the distance between certain places. He unfolded one at an end table and read the names, moved a finger at the road lines, the middle states between him and her sister.

47

HIS FATHER turned up when he came through the front of the house. The light above him was bright and felt fluorescent; his father's scalp slick pink beneath it.

You're dirty, he said.

He bent again over the black and white print magazine on the table in front of him. He turned a page and looked back up, pointed at Terry's knee busted red from practice.

Knee's broke.

Terry nodded, dropped his bag at the kitchen floor.

Is it the cap? Your patella?

It's just a grass burn.

Terry looked at his hands, lines stood white in the red of the palms; he closed them hard to fists a few times. The blood went to the tips of his fingers.

Those hurt?

Not so much.

He would not bathe, but ran water in the shower, anyway, because he liked the sound. He pissed at the drain and pulled the plastic curtain back when he finished. He took off the practice shorts and dropped them into a lump on the tile. He put on jeans, cupped water at his hands and rubbed his face. He took dope from an empty aspirin bottle in the medicine cabinet, dark, tight smoke he got from Curtis Rigby sometimes; it sparked and hissed when burned. He kept a small pipe John Michael Johnson sold him for a dollar inside the aspirin bottle, gold finished, shaped like a spark plug. He rolled it in one hand, metal cold against his skin. He opened the window and stuffed the bigger hole on the pipe, put the lid down on the toilet and sat there. He struck a lighter, bobbed it in front, pulled slow until the metal got hot on his lips and then he held the smoke until his eyes watered. He studied his knee; caked over, gone to scab. He pulled out pieces of grass left. The backyard outside the window was dark; on the north end of the roof, gutter rain fell through a floodlight. Small brown moths batted the windowsill. He blew smoke at some from the toilet, and one putted inside, drifted to the sconce over the medicine cabinet. The moth was thin, brittle, scrap tissue paper. He stood up, tapped the brushed glass covering the light. The moth flew out and landed on the white porcelain lip of the sink, fluttered terrible brown wings. He heard it thinking; not words, but something like the gray hiss wind put to trees when it blew hard. He put an index finger soft under one of the moth's wings, and it stepped between the first and second knuckle, stayed there still for a moment.

Benjamin Webber didn't say a word when he came back to the kitchen and told him he was ready to go. Terry was high, beaten, sure the air moved at his father's head and shoulders, sure he heard songbirds turned to smoke and crying inside the chimney.

Terry watched houses squat and brick on the way to the church.

What are you thinking about? his father said.

Terry didn't know how to answer. He didn't want to talk; nothing came of words neither one knew the meaning of. The road fell beneath them. Terry put a hand on the door latch. The grass burn throbbed on his knee. He winced.

Fuckall, he said.

I feel a little sad, his father said. Not sure why, really.

The tires caught another hole. Terry turned the radio louder. His father let it be for a moment, then twisted the knob back down.

You mad?

No.

Did you use soap?

What?

In the shower before.

Yes, I used soap.

You don't smell so good.

Neither do you.

Did you change clothes?

Stop with those goddamn questions already.

Maybe wash them again.

Both were quiet then for a few minutes, the streetlamps passed burn marks.

You miss that girl, his father said.

Some.

Terry didn't know how to miss her; she was there some weeks, for only a few moments. Sometimes he didn't know if she was anything at all, but something maybe he came across during sleep.

His father followed a house with his eyes when they passed.

Every day when I went to school I walked by this river, he said. In the mornings it was green, bright green sometimes, like algae in a swamp.

Terry scratched at his knee through the jeans.

But then in the afternoon, when I came back along that same river, it was red.

There's no such thing as water like that.

What do you know about it?

I'm just saying.

In all your fourteen years of fucking expertise.

Almost sixteen, dammit.

Terry scraped the grass burn on his knee with his fingernails, the throb gave to the scratch, and when he stopped it went back the other way.

I know when your birthday is. Two months you'll be sixteen.

Benjamin Webber changed hands on the steering wheel, left to right, wrist settled above the finger grooves. He looked quick to the passenger seat, square chin banded in yellow streetlight, and then he turned back.

Stop picking your goddamn knee, he said.

It's eight months anyway, not two, Terry said.

I knew that.

You didn't.

Terry leaned back, put a hand over his eyes and shut them. He pictured the pain in his knee, growing then, a red sun, and he focused on pushing the edges of it, shrinking it to nothing, but it stayed, and grew brighter.

Goddammit.

You've got a mouth like a damn pirate.

Just stop man.

I told you a valuable story.

Tell me what it means then.

Maybe nothing. Or, you know, whatever you want. The fact that a river was one color in the morning and another in the afternoon? Sometimes the world goes against what you've got set in your mind, you know, the path you've laid out for things. See I was little. Second grade, maybe third. I didn't understand downriver there was a factory spitting out dye every day at noon.

Terry put his face to the window and the dark trees passing. He thought to speak, but did not.

The church was brick and Episcopal, stained, glowing, named for a saint, or many saints, and he didn't mind it then because it was quiet, and he was high, and there was a great deal of color.

He sat with his father in a pew near the back, listened to the priest and long prayers everyone stood up to say. Terry couldn't understand any of it; communion of saints, resurrection of the body, right hand of God the father almighty, the quick and the dead and all that. He read the origins of songs from the list in the back of a hymnal; Danish, Korean, Welsh. He scribbled on the bulletin with a pencil from a slot on back of the pew, and then he wrote fake names on small cards used to request membership, general information, or a pastoral visit; Copernicus Donleavy, Roscoe Barakas.

The priest spoke low and even up front, palmed a small brass bowl. He said the ashes filled inside were made from burnt greens used at Christmas to decorate the sanctuary during advent; the big tree and the smaller ones, wreaths tied with wire and ribbon at the doors and the altar rail. He faced the small table below the pulpit. The ones he named stood up from the pews and walked silent to the front; he gave one the heavy brass candlesticks, another one the cross, and then he folded the green veneer cloth from beneath all three like a flag and handed it over; at each one he said our lord is dying. These are his limbs, he said, this is his heart.

He stood in line behind his father, watched his shoulders click beneath the white oxford dress shirt, one of two he owned, both of them old, full of starch and sweat, stained yellow at the neckline and on the chest. His face was newly shaved, hot water pink. Terry felt at his chin and cheeks, the sharp hair come in a little, wondered how the body knew when, how much, how to stop.

The priest spoke of dust, and when they got to the front of the line he crossed their foreheads with ash; when they were back in the pews he said our lord has begun the long walk, the long cold walk, and he does it every year, our lord, every year he sees his death, and he dies anyway, and then he does it again forever.

Benjamin Webber opened the front door, and Terry went inside. He rubbed his forehead and looked at his fingers. His father still had the lopsided and flaking cross above his eyes. He closed the door.

You shouldn't rub it off.

Terry stopped in the hall and looked back at him.

It's dirt.

It's not. It's not at all.

O N A Tuesday the team ran one mile. During drills he kicked with the dirty looking kid.

I'd like a cigarette, the dirty kid said.

Terry kicked the ball flat and straight.

I'd like a cigarette please.

The dirty kid spoke to the air. He let the ball get past, turned on his left heel and took a step, and then he brought it in and kicked it back. He turned his face and looked at some of the others. The coach yelled at them while they kicked. Terry saw a scar on his forehead, a skinny, jagged white line moving from his left eyebrow to the opposite temple, glossed in the light. Terry figured with all the weeks gone by the kid had seen his hands.

You can't smoke here, the dirty kid said. You can smoke everywhere in Russia, hospitals, even. That's the thing.

Why don't you go on and move then? Terry said.

All I need is the money.

The ball passed between them. By then Terry forgot anything he liked about the game. He had played a year some time back, quit, and none since, but on the sideline, during the second scrimmage in two days, he thought it was watching he liked, sitting crossleg on the sideline; calm grace in the ball's movement over field, through air and light.

Where did you come from, anyway? the dirty kid said.

Issaqueena.

That's upstate?

Three hours, a little more.

I was born in Atlanta, near the baseball field, I think.

I've never been there.

There's a building with a gold roof. The capitol, so they say.

Both were quiet a few moments, and then the dirty kid pointed at a tall gangly one who kicked a ways off, near the treeline. He bent down and set a ball carefully in place on the grass. He backed up a few feet, dropped his head, stepped quick and put his foot hard against the white and black checked rubber. The ball ran fast over the ground, popped at the ruts. The other one, ten feet off, gathered it in and held the ball still at his arches. The tall gangly kid bent down and picked something from the field. A ream of smoke came from his head. The other kid then sent the ball hopping back, came over and bent to the ground, same spot as the tall gangly one. After a few moments smoke came from his head, too. Both of them, Terry and the dirty kid, stared that way.

Are they smoking? Terry said.

Looks like it.

You just said you couldn't.

It's not cigarettes, fool.

Oh.

The ball passed him, and went toward another set of kids kicking, the whole swath of them on the field. Someone behind said, wake up.

Terry didn't play during scrimmage, and was glad of it. The sun had gone cold, and everyone on the sidelines wore new navy sweatshirts. He threw his in a brown metal dumpster in back of the vocational building. The dirty looking kid was on the ground beside him watching the game, and the tall gangly kid sat next to him. There were some others who never played slouched on both sides. The coach stood a few feet away. He turned back from the field and looked down at them.

Are you watching this?

They all nodded.

Pay attention, hippies.

He turned back to the game. The dirty kid put his middle finger on his forehead and looked at the coach's back.

I got your hippie. Damn pirate.

The tall gangly kid laughed, and Terry did, too. He quickly put a hand at his mouth. The laugh surprised him; he'd felt nothing like that in his throat for a long while. The dirty kid stared at the coach's rounded back.

Sonofabitch can't tell me that.

A cigarette the coach dropped was still burning. The dirty kid checked to see if he was still turned to the game. He leaned back and picked it up and took a drag. He thumped it down and exhaled. The wind took the smoke away from them, back toward the school.

There wasn't any avoiding the fact of them; after scrimmage they stood beside his window. Terry rolled it down halfway. Noah had a cigarette in his mouth already; Francis held a pack close to the jamb. Terry got out, followed them across the lot to a white two-door and got inside.

They sped past dead soy and cotton, the machine works, the red tin volunteer fire station. Terry rode in the back.

Noah's car had a low spoiler on the trunk. The trunk antenna was rusted, broken a point halfway up.

Francis sat in the passenger seat. His hair was long, and matted, the color of dried leaves, looked sealed with spit or petroleum jelly. He twisted pieces with an index finger, pulled them to his mouth and chewed the ends.

They parked at an unfinished drive at the back of the neighborhood, dead end on woods, and two framed houses each side, wooden bone and pink cotton, and red and black wire.

Noah took a joint from the glove box. He put a match on the end and pulled, held his breath when he spoke.

That's a nickname?

What? Francis said.

Not you, man. I know about your name already. Terry.

It's not from that saint, Francis said. I'm not one for animals so much. That saint, he liked animals.

Francis turned at the backseat and looked at Terry.

It's some actress my mom liked actually, he said. But she made it for a man, changed the last letters and all.

He turned back and pointed at Noah.

He's named for that guy in the bible. The one with that boat. There was a flood, right, a rainbow or something, and he was like nine hundred and fifty years old.

It was my grandfather's name, man.

Well he was named after that bible guy, then, with the white beard and all those animals. I think they wore robes. Probably he had a staff, and like forty children or a hundred.

People don't live nine hundred and fifty years.

They did then.

No they didn't, man. They just kept age different.

Years were worth more?

No.

Well?

Maybe a year was a month, or twenty days, or something like that.

I don't believe that.

Like I said, it was my grandfather's name, and he, I'm telling you, never set foot inside a damn church.

My grandfather called Jesus the Hypostatic Union.

Francis leaned over his knees at the floorboard. Noah looked at Terry in the rearview. He shook his head. Francis came up from the floor and kept his face at his lap. He worked on something at his kneecaps.

He was a doctor, my grandfather.

They passed the joint. The car filled with smoke. Noah put the joint out on the dash and kept the roach. They lit cigarettes; Noah's face rued at the trees in front.

Tasos died, he said.

Francis looked up quick, then back at his lap, pulled on three small tin hoops, key rings laced together, and tried to get them apart.

That weightlifter? he said.

Corman said he jumped out the back of a truck.

Bit to the right side of his mouth, the ash on Noah's cigarette crawled back some, then stayed, and then it burned back some more.

He tried to choke me once, Francis said.

Somebody else said he just fell over the side and got up under the tires. It like, took his legs off.

He was a damn pimp.

What kind of name is Tasos? Terry said.

Spanish, Francis said.

He's fucking Mexican, Noah said.

I just said that.

Noah pushed his cigarette at the ashtray beneath the radio. He got out another and mouthed the end to the popped car lighter, wire face hot orange from the battery. Francis threw the tin rings on the floor of the car; broken twigs and driveway flagstone caught in deep cigarette burns on the green floor mat.

Dammit, Francis said. I can't ever get those things apart.

It was a toy, a puzzle.

That goddamn Warren can do it, Francis said.

He put his face on the window. They kept smoking and then were quiet.

You ever seen a ninja ball? Francis said.

Noah looked at him.

I've heard of ninja stars.

Francis turned around to the backseat. He looked cold and sure.

You? he said.

Terry shook his chin, put his left hand to the door latch and lifted it some, and then he let it go, brought the hand down to his lap and raised the other one and pulled on his cigarette.

Nah, he said. I've never heard of those. Only ninja swords. And those sticks connected by chains they swing around.

Francis turned back to Noah.

Stars aren't even close to the same thing, he said.

Alright, Noah said.

You can only throw those at people, he said. They're like little knives. Haven't you ever seen any movies? Sometimes I think you're a foreigner. Ninjas throw balls down, smoke comes out and so forth. I got some from the flea market. We could use them to escape from something.

Terry started to twitch a strange way. He couldn't figure his movements, white fast and random, like tiny clouds exploding, or cotton heads chewed by a grasshopper swarm.

Are you from Bogotá or something?

What?

The capital of Colombia, man. Don't you pay attention in map class?

I hate it.

Well, I do. I pay attention all right.

In the rearview Noah scratched his head, eyes the color burnt red rock, streetlamp behind them a match burnt out.

I'm not out to hurt anyone is all, Francis said. We all keep hurting each other really bad, and we should stop.

Terry was having a hard time blinking his eyes.

49

FRANCIS WANTED some beer on Sunday. They drove to the border because of the blue laws and stopped at a filling station two miles after the green sign for North Carolina. Francis came out of the store and held six at the plastic tie, dropped the balled receipt in the parking lot, opened the door and sat back down inside the car. They made back south across the line and stopped a half mile past because the tower was sixty feet above the road and the top was a sombrero made of bright colored lights, and because Noah said, if God lived anyplace, it was there, or somewhere very close.

The tower was the centerpiece of the complex, a half-mile stretch of shops and restaurants cast bright colors; pink and green, blue and orange and yellow, built to look like desert missions. But in the weak light, when Noah passed the entrance and drove the gullet and the storefronts ticked close at both sides of the car, the paint jobs looked dusted, color muted behind a white coat of dust from the interstate. The head of the tower was built in the shape of a sombrero, and dotted with colored lights, green and yellow and white and red and orange, bright over the empty shops selling coffee mugs, baby spoons, stick puzzles, dice, picture key chains, ashtrays, live hermit crabs, piñatas and yardsticks to go with, knives and conch shells, penny rockets and roman candles and smoke bombs and sparklers and one knee-high fuse rocket with a plastic blue tip they called the gravedigger.

They paid a quarter, stood shoulder close and rode a metal box like a dumbwaiter to the top of the sombrero tower. Terry put his hands at the bars. The gears below turned a hard sound, and the metal wire on top scratched at the pulley. He watched the ground drop away.

The bill was a circle platform, and wide, big enough for twenty more. There was no one else. Noah put a finger in his beer can and wet the end. He touched a green bulb. It hissed.

Shit. It's damn hot.

It's a light bulb, Francis said.

Terry walked one lap on the platform. He squinted his eyes south at the light a white halo over the road and over the trees, put his hands on the black rail. He looked north; town lights the same; dumb, white. What he thought was, lean over at the dark. He dreamt times that he flew. Whole dreams felt a year, and he woke tired, shoulders sore, hours afterward looked at birds, great sadness in his throat. He kept his hands on the rail, and put his feet at the first bar and pushed up. The air felt good, cool at his face. His shirt bunched at the back and Noah yanked him down.

Get down man, Noah said.

Terry shook himself out a little. He brushed at the front of his shirt. Noah went back to where he and Francis stood and thumped a cigarette over the rail. Terry went up beside them. They lit a joint and passed it.

Fuck the Eiffel tower, Noah said. I won't ever go. Too fucking high.

Terry spit over the rail. Halfway down he couldn't see it anymore.

My uncle went there, Francis said. He brought me this plastic bird. You turned a switch near its ass, and it flew around. But the wings didn't last, they were this thin stuff. They just broke off after a little while.

I hate France.

You ever been?

No.

All those sonsofbitches smoke cigarettes.

My grandfather was there in the war. He said they're nice mostly, said he went on this girl in a windmill, with like, tulips all around it.

I can't trust a beret. I can't trust, like a country with nothing but stupid white people, like a whole place populated by rich, tennis playing dickheads.

I hate white people, Francis said.

Me too.

Noah and Francis drank a beer apiece and threw the cans over the railing. They took the cage down, then Terry left them and paid another quarter to go back up. Noah and Francis watched him rise, frayed wire over the dumbwaiter creaking like blackboard chalk and pulling him up; Noah said hurry up, man, and his voice got smaller; Francis bent down and picked at something in the grass. On the deck Terry listened close; strained engines, rushed air from cars shot past north and south, white highbeams, red brakelights, blurred yellow headlamps.

50

TERRY GOT up early and went into the kitchen. Benjamin Webber was sitting at the kitchen table, shoulder line like a headboard over the ladder back chair. He drank black coffee from a white mug, flying green and red duck curved at the face. His eyes were fixed at the window over the sink, the last shrug of blue hour, open catalogue in front of him.

All these damn redbirds, he said.

He shook his head back and forth. Terry stood over and looked at the catalogue. It was filled with different types of seed and bird feeder; post, box, cake.

I don't know about redbirds, Terry said.

I got someone over tonight. A woman friend of mine.

This was not unusual. His father entertained women periodically, but none of them ever stayed around long. He raised the mug and tipped to drink.

I got school today, Terry said. I'm going to school.

Go on then, his father said.

He knocked the mug a nod at the door.

In the driveway his car faced the sun. He watched it grow. Light warmed the vinyl.

In Geometry Mr. Noise drew powder blue squares on the chalkboard and pointed at them, spoke with his back turned.

Rhombus, he said. The plural is rhombi. That would be more than one rhombus. Like cacti. Or cumuli.

Francis sat two seats ahead. The roof of the classroom was particle-board, sectioned into squares at slim metal beams. One part at the back got wet and fell through, broke pieces on the floor, and then more of it fell down to the pile. Francis turned around, and threw Terry a crumpled piece of notebook paper. He looked down; a picture of two pigs drawn in pencil. Francis signed his name in cursive at the bottom. One pig was dressed in a tuxedo and the other a fancy dress. The pigs had curly tails. Terry laughed, high and sharp, and then Francis laughed. Mr. Noise turned around and put his eyes on their row; for a few moments he studied them.

Go and get to the corner, Mr. Noise said.

He pointed with both hands, like he led a plane to a landing strip.

They stood quiet a few minutes at separate corners, kept their faces on bends in the wall. Francis spoke low from one side of his mouth. Terry couldn't figure how to talk so the teacher wouldn't hear.

Mr. Noise is a funny man, he said. All those fucking shapes. It's bizarre.

Terry listened to papers folded, or turned over, the clang of chalk at the blackboard. Mr. Noise moved from talking about squares to triangles; some of the ceiling fell and landed on Francis's head.

Son of a bitch, he said.

Mr. Noise told them both to turn around.

Stop it, he said.

Something fell out of the ceiling and hit me, Francis said.

I saw it hit him, Terry said.

It won't hurt you, Mr. Noise said. It didn't hurt, did it?

Not really.

Be quiet, then.

Come on, Francis said.

Terry saw a girl that sat in front turn around with some of the others. He didn't know her name, but he thought she must be rich or something; she was fixed up, blond hair brushed light and straight, like a steel combed mane on a show horse. She wore a dark gray sweater and black pants, yellow ribbon tied prim tight at her neck. She turned back to Mr. Noise and moved a hand behind her head, stuck her middle finger up and held it that way and then she brought the hand back around in front.

Francis looked at her hard. Terry saw a polished gold pin at her chest the size of a driver's license. He squinted, made the words perfect attendance cut to the face. The girl was still looking at Francis. She stuck a tongue against one cheek and pushed it out, and then she mouthed shithead at him. Francis spoke loud, almost a yell.

I'm tired of this, he said. That's enough goddammit.

Mr. Noise turned around quickly, forehead lines pinched angry red.

Leave now, he said.

He pointed at the door to the classroom.

Principal Lemon, he said. Right now.

Come on, man, Francis said. Let's go out back and roll a number, sort this out? What do you say?

Mr. Noise huffed, gritted his narrow mouth, crossed his arms at his chest and then let them down, one armpit chalked a sky blue half moon on his white dress shirt.

I'm just kidding, man, alright? Francis said.

He held up both hands, fingers spread five points.

No harm done, Francis said. I'll leave.

Francis moved, got halfway to the door, but then he stopped and looked at the girl again. She mouthed something else. Francis shook his left hand at her.

You shut the fuck up, Francis said.

Mr. Noise's cheeks went bright, a drunk, whiskey flush; he clenched the chalk stub to a fist with his left hand, fingers ashed baby blue when he rolled it back and forth.

Leave, right now, he said. I mean it.

It's not fair, Francis said.

He put his hands on his hips, pointed to the girl.

She gives me the finger and I'm going to see the fucking principal? Tell me how that works? Do your job man.

5 1

THE COACH said they were bad players, told them to go two miles, and when they got done with that he sent them another two. At the first corner Noah said, fuck him, fuck him and all his coach clothes. Terry's chest and legs burnt, and his throat felt like it might close. He wondered how it'd be, like this maybe, tight chest and throat, or something else, like lying down, or more quickly even, eyes shut, the moment a word shapes in the throat. He kept running and got the asthma inhaler from his waistband and put it to his mouth and held it in.

On the drive home he saw Alice Washington standing on top of a house and her arms spread wide, yellow light all around her, and many blue flowers. A car blew its horn and shook Terry's head. He tried. He couldn't get her back.

52

THE COACH said if they didn't win, they never would. Dillon County was the worst he knew of; they wore football cleats, used cardboard for shin guards. He made them stand a circle around him before the game, walked a short line and looked hard at their still faces.

Play under control, he said. Break legs, dammit. Show these fuckers what's what.

Dillon County scored the first goal just past twenty minutes into the first half, a low runner toed to the right bottom corner. The coach went down to his knees and pounded the dirt with both fists. He pulled a kid named Merrill, and he sent another in. Merrill went to the water cooler, filled a cup and turned it over his head. The coach stood in front of him and pointed at his chest, whispered a snarl. Merrill turned to go at the field, and the coach took him by the shoulder. He looked hard at him again; Merrill nodded, bent down and tied a cleat, pulled his socks high and stood up. Coach pointed to the field.

Go dammit, he said. This is your job. This is your call.

Merrill turned his eyes down, knocked the ground with the tip of one cleat.

Merrill went midfield, stayed with Dillon County's one good player, the lanky fast kid that scored first. Merrill drifted back a little. The fast kid crossed midfield, caught the ball inside of his left foot, ran a slant to their sideline. Merrill slid at his legs, and then the fast one was up in the air, and then he was twisted on the ground.

At home Terry opened the window in his bedroom and sat beneath it. He spoke to her.

I'll seek you there, he said. In the still part of the afternoon. In the dry wind. Would you show me your face? Could I touch your dress?

The neighbor's tabby was plaintive, stalking redbirds in the yard, head jutted over pansy and marigold, butterfly in her mouth.

53

TERRY BOUGHT a pack of trucker speed for fifty cents at the service station on Irby. The package had a man with a mustache standing on the front who wore a black cowboy hat, a black, point collar shirt and smiled. There was a semi behind him, smoke come from exhaust pipes either side of the cab. Terry got back into the car. Benjamin Webber pulled off. Terry tore the pack at the top of the wrapper; three pills inside. He chewed one, small and white, crossed at the center. His father looked over.

What you got? he said.

Vitamins, Terry said.

His father held a soda over to him. Terry took a swallow, washed it around at his cheeks and cleared his mouth of the crushed powder.

Benjamin Webber drove them through a boarded-up town called Greeley; on the street cotton turned dry and gray, and some buildings missed walls, and some had gone to vine; trees grew on the roof of the old hotel, roots busted the awning. There were crows flying. They landed on roofs and power lines, dropped on fields and ate the ground.

The man on the corner past the hotel was black eyed. He wore a military hat with brass pins, held cardboard signs, shoulder level, painted crows; one had red eyes, and carried a shovel with its yellow feet. Terry was confused by the man, the way he hunched and sang, shoulders and head dotted bird shit.

Benjamin Webber slowed the car beside him and rolled down the passenger side window. Terry didn't want to talk to the man.

Man, come on, he said. Just keep going.

I want to see what this turkey wants.

Roll your own side down then, man.

Benjamin Webber leaned over Terry toward the window.

Just go, Terry said.

The man stood just past the window. Terry understood his father set his mind at seeing this thing to the end. The man smiled terribly, and didn't speak. He bobbed and held up a sign. Terry stared and didn't move, smelled him over the frame; fire, urine, paint. The man wore sunglasses, black and square, the kind Terry saw on old people in wheelchairs, or like ones who did metallurgy. Terry saw his eyes move behind the plastic, wobbled, both gone separate of the other; one pushed the top of a lid, the other strained toward the temple. The eyes scared him, shot a lump up his back, and he started to squirm. The seatbelt felt very tight, and bigger than before, metal clasp at his hip heavy and blunt. Terry pulled it away from his chest some and kept turning his head from the man to his father.

Fuck, man, he said. What are you doing?

His father's eyes were fixed, unwavered, everything in him, blood and bone, pushed toward a moment, and it came, the air sped, his father left the car, noise of all the world so much, so loud he couldn't sort one sound from any other; he thought it something like going blind.

His father got the man by the shoulders and turned him around and threw him at the sidewalk, all one motion, and then he stood over and pointed down at him harshly, forearm, crooked finger clenched on the end. He put a foot to his ribs and stood over him again, and then he leaned over and jerked the bundle of painted signs and stood up and threw them spinning at the street with the cotton.

The dead man was sixty-eight. Benjamin Webber found him at work, at his new plant, Purcell Uniform, sat down in the break room, black lunch pail open at his lap, one eye closed, the other a squint. The body was watched over in the old man's house. In the main room there was a large stone fireplace burning high and orange. At one side of it the old man's body lay flat on a long sheeted table. Terry got close to the table, and then he turned away quick, and left the room. He chewed more of the speed in the hall, ladled a small plastic cup with red punch and drank it in one turn, and then he filled it again and drank it all and set the clear plastic tumbler on the table.

Benjamin Webber came after him, squinted his eyes and took his arm in the hall. His father held him at the bicep, and spoke close to his ear.

Right now you're doing this, he said. You hear me?

Terry looked down on the powdered face of the old man; hair slick wet and white, combed straight back, scalp still a bit pink underneath. His lips were thin, not smiled, or turned down, just a flat line painted lipstick beneath his nose. He still dreamt of certain things; Terry saw that. He wanted to touch his lips, wanted to sit him up on the table. The man with the signs rose up in his head screaming, his father perched and stomping above, cardboard turned in the air like shingles broke during thunder. He couldn't tell why; looking twisted his face up. He wished to cry, or scream, but neither came, only the sure fact of his father next to him, speaking close in his ear, saying nothing. Terry jerked his arm away, and his father took it again.

Let go, Terry said.

He shook it again. His father kept his hand. Terry could feel heat there, blood in the fingers pried at his arm. He turned then and looked him straight, kept his eyes still, focused a cold fury. Benjamin Webber hunched his brow to lines.

Terry went upstairs to the old man's room. He stood in the doorway, light from the hallway at his feet and into the darkened room. He turned the light switch; framed pictures, chest level on the dresser of the old man and what looked his wife and children. He unde\rstood he'd never have a thing like that, pictures or people, a dresser or a house. He understood he'd be an old man, that he would carry much hurt, but that he'd be alone, watching others, waiting on someone to come who never would. He understood this was his lot. He turned off the light.

Terry stepped further into the room and opened cabinet drawers, put two bottles of pills at his jean pockets; from a jewelry box beside the bed he took eight silver dollars, a gold wedding band.

54

THE GAME was at seven, beneath lights, in a railroad town called Seneca, an hour and a half west of Echota. The road emptied, the sun weak. They passed a broken house set alone in a field. Francis said an old man lived there, said he killed his family, eight of them, and once a week, on Saturday, brought the gravestones from the backyard into the house and washed them with a toothbrush in a white claw-foot tub. They passed billboards on the highway; on one an elderly man and woman bore teeth, pedaled a red two-person bicycle on a path through fall leaves.

The high school stood all alone in cleared woods. Noah wedged the car between a row of three classroom trailers and a wide brick building. They kept the windows up, smoked a joint. Terry carried the plastic radio along to play the tape, kept it beside him in the backseat. They listened to a record by the Clash called *Sandinista!* They smoked a few cigarettes after the joint. The music hummed, made his eyes blink a flutter; he felt every vein. What he thought was, cut my wrists, I'll bleed ash, smoke.

The first goal came fifteen minutes in the first half. Noah got up from the bench, went over to the water cooler and came back with two short paper cups filled with a bright yellow drink, handed Terry one of the cups and then sat back down. He bent forward and reached at his sock, put a blue pill to his mouth. He dropped another in the grass next to his foot. Terry reached down and picked it up, size of a thimble.

Halftime coach made them sit a circle around him. He stood over them with his hands at his hips and mumbled. Terry didn't listen, went warm from the pill. He pulled grass from around his knees and threw it back down. He put some in his mouth and chewed. He built a small teepee with some twigs and it fell over. The world took a kind light, soft, blue, pale like through stained glass. Terry held his right hand straight in front; a stillness there he never felt, in all of him, eyes and ribs, legs and breath.

The second half started on midfield. Terry stayed sitting crosslegged on the ground near the bench, head lolled with the game and the lights, the grass growing at his thighs. He thought of a blue-eyed, charcoal cat from Issaqueena. It didn't look him in the eye, but he knew it remembered his face. He found a dead bird in the storage shed, a few days later a squirrel, then a small, stump-eared rabbit, none of them mauled like the ones he saw the cat catch and toss around, but just dead, sat careful, a gift, he thought, maybe just another way to speak.

55

THEY SPENT hours at Orangepants, a pool hall and fish market, left between games for the alley in back of the place. He felt dark, sad, and his eyes watered, and they left him in the alley in the dusk light hung over. He pulled hard on the last of the joint, propped himself at the wall, stayed there and watched the light go.

Noah beat a big man and motioned across the table for his money, ten dollars. The big man was a Lumbee. He put a leg up on the table, yanked the cuff past his ankle, deer knife stuck in the sock. He tapped on it, kept the leg on the rail.

Noah asked the Lumbee to go up front and buy them a box of malt liquor since they couldn't. He came back and opened the top flap, twelve short green bottles, and then he spoke of his tribe; he was the one that remembered the true name of the big river, but during spring, the water spilled the banks, settled peat black and still, and afterward it was something else, water he couldn't name.

They ran across Irby with bottles wrapped in their jackets. A few of the bottles fell and broke on the road, and they laughed because the night was cold and blue. They kept a sprint to Noah's car, drove a few blocks to a red brick church and parked in the lot behind it. Francis knew the place; no one allowed there past dark.

Francis got out. He drank a bottle, two swallows, threw the empty against the wall overhand, like a fastball. The bottle yelled on the brick. Terry and Noah went to drinking theirs, and then Noah broke one, and then Terry did, and then all of them threw bottles three, five, eight. They leapt, arms up, at the cold clear night and the gasoline in their hearts; glass green in the air, busted on the ground.

Then the sirens were all around them.

Terry went to run, and then he stopped.

They stood in a line, held their hands above their heads. Two of the policemen shone flashlights inside Noah's car, bright as spot lamps for blinding deer at the popped trunk; gun in the glove compartment, under a frayed eastern state highway map, the car title, and lug wrench. One of them dug it out and held it up. It was square, looked like a plastic starter gun. Noah dropped his eyes and wagged his chin, orange hair a kerchief over his forehead. His father left the gun; nights he drove to the bar and hovered at drinks with other men and women who didn't remember what morning smelled like. On his way home, late, toppled fences, dogs, left the car on the side of the road, skewered on a front yard. Noah nodded to the gun.

Gun's not mine, he said.

None of this seemed true to the policemen. One asked for other weapons. Francis pointed to the car ten feet off. The one holding his arms behind let go and walked him over. Francis leaned down and reached under the passenger seat, raised back up holding a bundle.

Then the policemen put them facedown beside the car and locked their hands. They laughed, lit a few of the smoke bombs Francis fished from beneath the seat, and dropped them hissing on the lot. Terry lifted his face to see the smoke and the policeman pressed his boot harder at his back.

Stop moving, he said.

This is a bunch of shit. What kind of operation are you running here?

The policeman put a hand to the back of Terry's head and pushed his face down, gravel spiked to his cheeks.

They put the three of them at the backseat and drove to the sheriff's department and locked them in one of the two cells for drunks. One of the policemen called them ruffians, and then he called them vagrants. There was a toilet in the cell, benches on two sides, walls painted yellow, names scribbled in black pen and lead. There were chipped places on the slick gray floor like liver spots. They sat, feet down, and none spoke. End of the hall a door slammed, then boots, loud and final, stomped toward the cell. The policeman who put Terry down turned the lock and slid the bars, motioned for Noah and Francis to stand and they did. He pointed them down the hall. Francis moved past the open cell door then stopped. Noah lingered inside the bars and looked down at Terry.

What do we do here? he said.

Terry shook his head and fumbled at his hands set between his thighs, bottom of his forearms close to the bent knees.

Go on, he said.

Noah pinched his eyes and stood mute.

I'll be alright, Terry said.

They called his house for an hour, and after another hour one of them let Terry from the block with a loud key and led him down the hall, and then he drove him home, when there stayed a few feet back and watched Terry turn the deadbolt. The house was dark. Terry switched on the light and pointed down the hall. The officer leaned his head past the doorframe and had a look.

I told you, Terry said.

The policeman looked again.

If he doesn't call man you know where I live alright?

The officer nodded.

Here man, if you don't believe me or whatever.

Terry went to his back pocket and dug out his wallet. He peeled the driver's license from beneath the plastic and held it to the policeman.

56

THE JUDGE gave them forty hours of community service; Noah read to children at the town library and picked trash in the yard. Francis painted the elementary school canary yellow. Terry came to the aluminum finishing plant at first light, and on the way he passed a graveyard for soldiers, the headstones small white tablets. At the north end a group of old buildings, weathered brick and white paint; during the states' war, one was a prison on the blue side. Terry listened hard, for chain rattle, for the sick and dying.

The plant was out on the old state highway, beside the county airport. He parked the car and studied the field next to the building, a deep stretch of cut grass between blacktop and control tower, rotted planes laid in rows after the great world wars.

He walked up and pushed the door at the front of the building, and it held and then he pushed some more and it scraped open. It was dim inside, an old airplane hangar open at both ends.

There were no shifts on the weekends; Monday the boxed aluminum shipped and the rigs shook impatient at the north end. He hole-punched a card past the front and set it to a slot, his last name penciled on top. He worked alone, punched holes to long and thin strips of aluminum used to stay carpet. He made boxes from sheets of seamed cardboard and staples and stacked the fresh punched aluminum to the boxes and stuffed the extra space in thin, pink paper. The sky was clear, and the sun high through holes rusted in the ceiling.

Terry came Tuesday, after practice and the main shift over and gone at three-thirty. It went dark. He spotted cats with no tails, leering at him from beams at the hangar walls. He left a bundle of punched aluminum on a sheet of the pink paper, went outside and gathered small rocks in the truck bay and came back through the front and threw them and scattered the cats and the rocks shook the metal.

He took a half hour for break. He went out back of the place and sat on a metal boat that faced the plane yard. He chewed a candy bar, and then he smoked a cigarette, and a few of the old planes were painted a new white, and someone stood beneath a bomber with no wheels, arm raised to the belly.

Terry went to him across the yard, and the kid didn't turn, not even when he stood a few feet close. He'd seen him at school a few times in the parking lot, sat down in the front seat of an orange hearse. He was shaped like a bulldog; flat shaved head, neck mostly shoulders. He held a square-headed brush and moved it careful over the underside of the plane, four cans of paint open in the grass around him, black shirt and jeans blotted white, bits of paint in his hair. He smoked a cigarette.

You're going to make a fire, Terry said.

The kid turned and kept the cigarette at his mouth and then he dropped the brush against a hip.

The fuck are you? he said.

His voice was even, unmoved. He raised the brush and went back on the plane.

I was just over there making boxes.

No shifts past three-thirty.

The judge put me there.

The kid blew smoke, thumped the butt under another plane.

Probably the same one put me here painting these fucking birds, he said. I'd beat the wrinkles out of that one. You steal something?

I was throwing bottles against that church downtown. They found a gun.

The kid dropped the brush and checked his hands.

Cats still there?

He bent down to a knee, wedged lids back on the cans.

I did summers in that plant, for pay, he said.

I've seen some. I throw rocks at their heads.

They're fast.

The kid put some things in a storage shed and kept an open can. He made to leave, and started at the highway, and then he threw a wide smile of white against the wing of one plane. Paint beaded and dripped, and then he dropped the can, spilled white on the old grass.

PRINCIPAL LEMON decided throwing bottles against a church was crime enough to kick them off, and coach sat them down after practice.

My hands are tied. Bound by a force which I have no control. I wish it were different.

Terry walked a field behind his father's house, busted heads of milkweed in the air. The dead light broke over the ground and farther the trees grew thick and the ground pushed up thorn and tight brush against his calves and the air dropped cold.

He found a rusted car shell, metal and sour vinyl, wheels gone, hood peeled one corner over the empty engine block, fallen limbs inside on the maroon seats, grass grown up through all of it. He pulled branches out. He scaled a window frame legs first, hands on the door. He sat down and put his hands on the rotten steering wheel. He tore foam from the seats. It broke dust at his hands. His breath fogged; he liked watching it frozen in the half light coming through rust holes in the roof and the split back windshield.

He climbed out of the car and stood in front of the engine block. He lit some old newspaper, got a bottle of lighter fluid from his jacket and pushed a stream at the flame. It caught blue, and the fire nodded, a bear pushed from sleep. He watched it for a moment, and then he dropped two red plastic lighters inside. They swallowed heat and trembled, burst a dull

thud. The fire caught grass and trash and branches and burned high orange. He warmed his hands, chewed trucker speed.

Past the fire and the far trees the sky lit green and sparked, risen light like
a star shot from the ground. Another light arced, pink this time, purple
the next, then blue, all hissed toward him, into the black and then down,
burning in the woods.

He kept the car between him and the lights and crouched at one side. He
stayed that way for a moment. It was quiet; he knew it was the Russians,
the red storm, fur-lined earflaps and sickles. It didn't matter. He knew for
a long time they were coming. For many years the actor president promised such a thing. Terry tapped his pockets for the knife and tried to hold
his words. He'd left the knife beneath his pillow.

Fuck all, he said.

There were fell branches in the leaves. He picked one up. It bent wet, and
he knocked it against the ground and it fell off at the middle. He pulled
one from the engine block, fire burning at one end, held it up high, a
torch.

The first one grazed the roof of the car and fell off behind him, and then
they came faster, splitting branches and pitching the high leaves. The
rockets were small, moved fast through the dark. Terry crouched, put his
eyes over the lip of the engine block and held the branch high in the dark,
the rockets still, then, and the trees silent. He waited, and the deep quiet
stayed, and he waited some more and then he stood up and held the lit
branch in front of him.

He saw it come; a hiss, soft and then loud and gathering speed, a burning
yellow spark through the dark and the woods. He watched it crash his
nose; the force of it sent him backward to the leaves and crossed his eyes,
his neck thrown back, nose cracked white, hot pain shuddered through
his cheeks.

Terry opened his eyes and twitched, looked up to the tops of trees. There
were voices nearby. He turned his head on the ground, the fire high again

at the block; beside the car, shaded outline of shoulder and neck. He
slowed his breath, worked his hands in the leaves for a branch he could
use as a club. He moved his legs. Leaves cracked and jostled. The near
voices stopped. He found a branch in the leaves, stayed on his back, dead
limp.

The legs got close enough. He swung the branch and broke it to one set of
knees; a yelp, then, and one of them dropped to the dry leaves. Terry
pushed up at his hands and got two steps on a run. The shirt bunched
around his neck, and he fell hard to his back. A set of knees pressed cap
point on his biceps, dark face above turned to one side, the other down in
the leaves and yelling. His nose beat hard. He felt the blood swell in his
cheeks. Eyes fixed to the weak light over the shoulders above him, he
made out the face some more; dark eyes, like mallets, head shaved an
army cut, widow's peak a knife tip. His shirt was black or blue, the word
FEAR pasted in sharp white letters on the chest. Terry remembered him
from the plane yard and shook his arms.

Come on, man, he said. The fucking airplanes remember?

The kid sitting on top squinted his eyes some more, loose and wet in
the sockets. Terry smelled drink on him.

The cats? The fucking judge? We talked, man.

Are you following me?

No, man.

The kid at the ground stood up, narrow shoulders, head cocked to one
side. He brushed his chest off, stepped close to them and stood over.

What are you doing out here? he said.

I built that fire, Terry said. I was just out here, man, smoking fucking
cigarettes. Man, come on.

Terry jerked an arm from under the kid's knees. The kid took his arm
with one hand and jammed the knee back down on top.

What are you two jackasses doing here? Terry said. You and fuckface
over there. It's not your woods, man, you don't own them. Get off, man,
fucking get off.

I don't know this person. Did you call me fuckface?

Terry's mouth was dry. He turned his head on the ground and spit at
his feet. Not much came out. The kid on top brought his right arm down
and gripped a hand wide at his jaw, thumb and fingers wrapped a smile,

ear to ear. It didn't feel like he meant to choke him. But then the hand clenched more. Terry knocked at the kid's forearm with the loosed hand, opened his mouth, and no words came out. The other one stood up, said Stop, fucking quit. He pushed the kid hard at the shoulders, and the hand left Terry's neck. He breathed in hard, turned on the ground to his chest. He pushed up on his hands and knees and stayed. The big one crouched low on his heels.

I remember you, he said.

Terry nodded, and then he spit.

I have this ghost in me sometimes, the big one said.

The big one rubbed his eyes with the butts of his palms, and then he stood and put a hand down and helped Terry up.

I thought you were Russians, Terry said.

No, the big one said. Just recreational fireworks is all. It's a hobby, I guess you'd call it.

He went with the two of them back over to the fire set in the engine block. Isaac Calendar was tall and skinny, head shaved both sides, long piece left in the middle, bent over his right eye. His head was cocked to one side. He wore a dark shirt that read SAMHAIN. Louden was bigger than Terry remembered. He stoked the fire with a stick. Isaac dropped a box of matches. The fire welled. They saw his face.

You get hit? Isaac said.

Somebody got hit, Louden said.

I hope they look as bad.

Terry's nose was swollen up to his eyes.

Wasn't a person, he said. One of those rockets.

Rockets? Isaac said. Like spaceships?

I don't know what it was. Something flying through the woods. It sounded like a rocket.

They looked him stone face for a few moments.

Louden spit some beer on the ground and wiped his mouth. Isaac got two sparklers from his jacket. He gave Terry the last handful of bottle rockets. Terry lit the fuses and shot them off at the woods. Isaac burned a sparkler and stared at the waved green bloom. They looked to Terry like a planet's birth.

I guess they're dangerous, Isaac said. People say that, but I've never seen it.

Louden shook his head at him.

Tell that to my old man. Ask him where his thumb is.

Where is it?

A bunch of pieces, man.

Terry slept with his nose throbbing and by morning it was fat and swollen to his cheeks. His father stopped him in the kitchen, studied his face and the gash there.

Go on and sit down, he said.

Terry sat down, leaned on the tabletop and rubbed his forehead. Benjamin Webber put ice from the tray to a plastic sandwich bag and twisted the top and tied a flimsy knot. He set it down on the table in front of Terry, ran water in the sink until it steamed and held part of a dishtowel beneath the steam.

Who got after you? he said.

He touched Terry's nose with the end of the towel. Terry winced.

Shit, man, careful. It was a bottle rocket.

His father dropped the towel to the counter and lifted the plastic bag filled with ice.

Hold this on your nose until it hurts, he said. It'll go numb after that.

Terry took the bag.

Like a damn firework thing? his father said.

That's what hit me.

Benjamin Webber smiled a little.

Playing a war then? he said.

No.

Just out of nowhere? That's what you're saying?

I am.

Benjamin Webber finished at the cut and went over and dropped the towel in the sink. He stayed looking through the window to the back and did not turn when he spoke.

Me and this woman, he said. That's nothing about anyone but me and her.

I understand that.

Sometime you'll know, this life, this one right here, it'll bleed you, son, if you don't make a spot.

Terry watched him close the back door and go outside. He thought of him sobbing, like a baby, remembered how it scared him. He remembered the burn marks in the wood floor. He went to his room, opened the window and smoked. The air moving past the house curled the smoke over one side of the window frame when he blew it out. He put a hand outside to feel it. He brought the hand inside, and then he lit one end of the gold metal pipe shaped like a spark plug. He pulled a long time and held it in. He coughed when he blew out and he kept coughing. He put a hand to his mouth and leaned over onto his thighs. When it left him he raised up, his father's head close to the bottom of the sill.

Come on out, he said.

Terry didn't move, or speak.

I don't give a shit, now, come on outside.

Benjamin Webber sat back pressed to an oak. Terry stood in front of him. His father looked up.

What do you want me out here for?

Sit down alright?

Benjamin Webber patted the dirt and Terry lowered down at one side of him and crossed his legs.

You got some more? his father said. What you had going in there?

Terry nodded, hesitated on his pocket for a moment and then he took out the pipe. He crammed the head full and gave it to his father. Benjamin Webber held it up, squinted his eyes and studied it for a moment in the light. He smiled.

Can I hold that lighter? he said.

Terry gave it to him. He stuck a flame and held it to the end and squinted his eyes to the head of the pipe. He blew out and coughed, put the back of one hand against his mouth.

I used to have one like this, he said. Or I'd roll up those joints sometimes. I had a wood pipe, too, from Africa.

He passed the bat and lighter over to Terry.

I had it for a while. It was my favorite. This shithead Frank, I can't remember his last name, Crory, maybe, rich white boy type, always playing

fucking golf or something you know, goddamn croquet, he wanted to go
off with this girl one night. He needed it, you know, so they could get high
and loose, and then he comes back a few hours later and gives it back. It
was cracked, split right down the middle, the whole way up. Done for
good.

Terry packed the head again and pulled smoke. He held it in, gave it
over once more to his father. Benjamin Webber took the pipe, held it
while he spoke.

When he's walking off, I say, Hey Frank, and he turns around, and I
hold the thing up. So the jackass just shrugs and starts to go off again.
Maybe I was feeling mad about something, I can't remember. I booked
right at him and got him by the shirt and turned him around, and still, he
shrugs. Next thing I'm jamming him up against a wall. I went to his pockets, I thought he might have some dope, maybe, some money to pay me
back, seeing as he's a fucking rich boy, but there's nothing. Nothing except a pipe like that.

Benjamin Webber held it up and then he gave it back.

Right in his front pocket, he said. It was gold, you know? I never saw
one like that. I said, Frank, I'm keeping this, and then I let him go. I
pushed him, I think. Maybe I slapped him.

You want more? Terry said.

I'm good.

Benjamin Webber patted his chest.

I'm high as a falcon, he said.

Terry got another hit and coughed. Benjamin Webber patted his back
like Terry saw women do to babies.

Frank, his father said. He did this thing, he'd tap you on the shoulder
in class, make a pistol with his fingers, move his thumb like the hammer.
He did it when you could see between a girl's legs, you know, said he was
shooting a squirrel.

What?

Nothing.

Benjamin Webber scanned the yard back and forth. Some small gray
birds knocked at a feeder and squawked. A few cardinals jumped among
them, stormed red and yelled, sprang away, and then did it again.

They like whatever seed you put out, Terry said.

Benjamin Webber nodded.

My old man liked to hunt, you know, he said. Anything. He shot all of it. Birds, though, most times. He took me with him some before he figured pretty quick I wasn't for it. He'd go for doves, but any kind that flew past he shot, so close sometimes they just popped. Gone. Nothing but some feathers left. And he laughed, too, was the strange thing. He used some long-barreled thing that was taller than me.

This one time, he helped me hold it, and we shot a dove from a power line. When it fell down we walked over. The gun shook even with my old man helping it was so big, but the shot didn't get the bird so well. Took a piece of its wing off. It was twitching around and blinking its eyes. The most scared thing I've ever seen, ever. These black eyes going back and forth and this sound coming out of it like a person crying. He reached down and took the bird and he showed me how to hold the body, around the wings so it couldn't squirm, told me to hit its head against my boot. I didn't want to, but I did, and the head didn't come off, and I tried again, and it still hung on and he kept saying do it again, do it again, but it wouldn't come off. I just kept going. Don't know how long it took. There was blood all over my pants and feathers stuck. Then its head popped off. The thing I couldn't let be, besides its eyes, was how corn came out of its neck after I knocked the head off, feed corn. The bird had just finished eating, I guess. It was just sitting there on the power line, resting, until we shot it.

Neither one of them said anything for a few minutes. After a while his father stood up slow and wobbled. Terry rose up quick and put a hand at his shoulder. His father put a hand on Terry and caught himself. He nodded, smiled some, and took his hand away.

I'm fine, he said. I'm good.

What was she like? Terry said.

Who?

My mother.

What do you mean?

I mean, did she like flowers?

Yeah.

What sort?

Petunias.

Petunias?

You like repeating things.

I know, man.

There were pink ones she liked.

Terry went inside and stood at the window. He watched his father in the backyard raised tall in the early light bowed through pine and over his shoulders, redbirds busy on seed, heads turned, splay of wings. Benjamin Webber crouched low, spilled seed from one hand to the ground. The birds dropped and huddled at his feet.

Terry put on earphones and turned a record up loud and listened until it was late. The record skipped, and the needle hung on the fourth song. He put the arm past the scratch. He didn't want to hear his father and his woman friend moving in the house. He took the headphones off and started watching a program about sharks and how they liked to eat people. He was close to sleep, eyes sunk slits. He nodded, and his chin dropped.

The doorknob rattled and it shook him awake. He fell off the bed and crashed on the floor.

There was a light knock. Terry stood up and went over to the door and put his hands and one ear against it. He listened for a moment, and then dropped to the floor. He saw two feet under the gap, toenails painted light blue. He thought for a moment what to say, and stood up.

Can I help you with something? he said.

The knock came once more, and he was confused, and then he unlocked the door and went over to a chair at the window and sat down.

Come in?

A woman with thick red hair smiled and pushed through the door and shut it behind. She had on loose dark brown corduroy pants, a hooded gray sweatshirt, MONTANA printed at the front. She moved a chair from another corner, brought it close to his. She turned it backward and sat down, leaned her chest and arms on the chair back.

Your father's asleep, she said.

Terry looked down at his feet.

Okay, he said.

I couldn't sleep, she said.

She tapped her hands against her thighs.

Can I have some of that?

She pointed to the pipe on his bedside table.

She laughed after the second pull, smoke piped from her nose and mouth. She coughed, patted her chest with one hand. Her eyes watered.

I like it when it gets right here, she said.

She put four fingers at the base of her ribs, told him she worked across the highway from a boat warehouse, in the head office of a company that manufactured hosiery and frozen desserts, wholesale. She gave people jobs; sometimes she took them away. Before that she worked with the records of an insurance company, and then later, at another job, she watched kids drive gasoline-powered miniature race cars and sometimes split their heads open.

I knew how to scuba dive, once, she said. I was very good at it.

She tapped her left ear.

I popped this one, she said. I went too deep.

She pulled one pant leg up to the knee, scar on the shin like a smile.

That's a tiger shark, she said. But just a small one.

She took a pull from the pipe and held it in. She blew out and stood up, made circles with her thumbs and index fingers and put them over her eyes like a mask, acted like she was swimming.

For a quarter mile the wide trunks passed by in clicks, high branches grown mesh over the road, yellow pass line in front fuzzed a seam. The moon broke through, put white and shaken spots to the blacktop. Cars were parked at both shoulders on the road, roofs sloped with the easy hills.

Noah thought there was money to be had. He wanted to sell a half ounce, make enough to buy more, pull some and sell the rest, and keep going as long as the cycle held. He put the car to a low gear, drove the line for a space. Terry looked at the oaks on the side of the road. The car slowed down, and he saw inside them, at the year rings older than money. He saw insects wailing on the leaves and in the bark; he saw heavy white owls standing mottled and blood flecked in hollow spaces in the trunks over tiny bones and tufts of hair. He used the asthma inhaler more times than he was allowed.

Francis pushed the radio down and turned his head to the back.

If you do it, like, a hundred times in a row, you get hallucinations, he said. Scientists say that. And, like, various industrialists.

A few miles passed. Francis spoke then on how his grandmother came from the Balkans.

Noah settled at the end of the line and parked the car. They went to the trunk. Terry knocked light at the rear glass. Francis looked up, and the trunk rose. Terry turned back to the front and waited, leaned over his thighs and squeezed the police knife cuffed in his right sock, blade end notched to his ankle like a pipe fitting. He pulled the cloth up tight over the knife and dropped the pant leg.

Noah pushed a tire one side and got the paper bag of dope from the hollowed space beneath. He put it to a back pocket. He looked at the tire again and punched the frayed rubber.

The houses in the neighborhood were old, wooden and brick, with sharp black iron fences. They walked beside the cars on the shoulder. Francis tapped hoods. Ahead of them a hearse was parked in the grass between the lined cars and the brick fence, its back hitch dropped. A few kids sat there, and some stood around like they warmed their hands at a fire. Music spit muffled and fast from the open hitch. A tall kid faced it. He had a military build; lanky and stern, wide backed. He put a fist hard against another skinny kid in baggy jeans beside him. The skinny one had a chain hung in a loop from one back pocket to the bend of his knee, arms inked to the wrists, hands a shocked white beneath blue and black line. He laughed, got hit again, and then winced and rubbed his shoulder. Terry remembered him from the woods; Isaac Calendar. The one sat to the middle of the hitch he recognized too; Louden; he looked a bulldog, a guard, thick neck and a flat head. The girl beside him had long hair, dark blond and straight, grown past her shoulders and over her back, pecking at the dip above her waist, skin pale in the streetlight. Terry thought about the story with the woman in the tower and her hair so long people used it as a ladder to reach her window. She wore baggy jeans, cuffs that draped wide over her feet and scuffed the ground. She wore a black shirt with BLACK FLAG pasted on the chest in white letters, bottom pulled tight at her back, twisted to a tail in front. Terry stared at the stretch of bare stomach, stared at her hips pushed against the waistline. He wanted to draw pictures, mark them as landmarks, continental divides.

Terry and Francis stayed back while Noah went over to the kids at the hearse. Noah took out the paper bag and handed some of the dope to a tall kid. The girl leaned back some and dug to a front pocket. She gave Noah a wad of folded bills, and he took the money, put the paper bag in his back pocket and nodded at the ones on the hitch and then he turned to leave.

Noah and Francis went first to the guesthouse. Terry followed close, and watched the backs of their heads. He stopped past the door and studied a small black piano when he took his eyes from the gloss on the lid, didn't see them in the smoke and room twitter; they were gone, or they were right beside him; face and light and voice spun together, and he couldn't tell the edge of anything. He leaned hard against the piano, felt like he would fall, and he was given to it, but his legs welled and he stood back straight. He had a bottle of malt liquor in one fist, his other hand to a pocket. He took the bottle to his mouth and drank. There were stubbed cigarettes and ash on the piano lid. He swept them to the floor.

A bony dark-headed girl from school was across the room, above heads, through smoke, her cheeks flushed pink in the light. Terry watched as if she were a bear. She held a small box and tipped the open end, threw red candy to her mouth. Her slim body turned through the smoke, her face clear and sharp in the squawk of voices in the room. She moved like a girl he watched in a talent show wearing a blue sequin dress, shone chain mail beneath hot lights on the stage. That one scared him, hurt his eyes she was so blue. The girl across the room turned her face at the corner where he stood, eyes poked big, and he tried to stay at them, but he couldn't; it was like watching the sun for too long or turning music to a blare. He turned away, pulled the snow hat down far at his forehead and stayed hunched to the piano, turned his head to the window behind him. A floodlight dropped yellow on the brick walk. Terry raised up and looked for the girl across the room. He couldn't find her; people in the guesthouse confused him, voices coupled with the music; they were so loud, and so many. The open heart of the room felt a question with no answer. He couldn't tell, right then, if he was dreaming.

Outside Terry walked past the hearse again and heard someone laugh. A bottle panged empty on the concrete. Noah and Francis were on the path at the north wall, a walkway lined with row plates, stone faces carved smiles and frowns, high bushes on both sides, leaves tipped red. Noah sat beside one bush and laughed. He was sweating, eyes puffed like he'd wept. Francis stood above him and peered down. His hair hung mostly over his face. Noah pointed down, to a streak of foam on the walk stone.

Francis told me to eat the roach, he said.

I said you could, Francis said. That's it. Nothing else.

Is that vomit? Terry said.

I just spit up some foam is all. I chased the roach with beer see. It was stuck in my throat. It's still on fire.

It wasn't on fire.

It was. I could feel it. Right here.

Noah put a finger halfway up his neck.

It burnt a hole I think, he said.

Noah clapped. Terry held a hand to him.

They went back for the front gate. Noah fell at the shoulder of a kid standing with his back to them, bowed him forward a step. Noah stopped, wobbled, calmly brushed the kid's shoulder with one hand.

Sorry, Noah said.

He brushed his shoulder again.

Okay, he said. All clean. No more tears.

The big kid turned around, took Noah by the front of his shirt and wadded it tight, pulled him up on his toes. The shirt stretched to rip at his back; Noah laughed.

You're mad, he said. I can see that now.

The big kid dug at Noah's back pocket, brown paper bag with the dope inside, got it out and held it wadded tight in a fist. Noah's shirt slacked and his heels dropped. He grabbed at the bag in the big kid's hand. The big kid knocked him away with the other hand, held the bag high over one shoulder. Terry felt the knife pressing sharp against his ankle, thought, maybe, this was a good time to bring it out, with this trouble. He went down to a knee, pulled the side of the pants leg up and worked the sock down over the head of the knife. Francis was at the big kid, going after the bag. Another kid, almost as big as the other one, but slim and lanky like a midfielder, stood a few feet away, pulling a baseball cap low, dragging the bill up and then back down, big hands flapped stout from his small wrists, like heavy gloves on a flyweight. They tossed the stash high between them, a game of catch, father and son in a yard lobbing a baseball. Francis and Noah lurched back and forth. The first one stopped after the fifth high-arced toss between them, took Noah at the back of the shirt and planted him to the ground. Noah's head made a dull sound on the brick when he hit the walkway, ear and temple first. He rolled over and palmed his head like they did on bomb drills at school. The other kid grabbed Francis from the back, long arms around his chest, held him for a moment and then put him down hard. Francis came down on his knees and cocked wrists.

Terry unfolded the knife, held it blade down and stood up, eyes pinned, slanted in some old fury, and walked fixed, blade bore a point to the ground. He raised it up, held his arm straight, and shoulder level, walked like he thought one of those explorers did when reaching new land.

The first kid, the big one, sat on top of Noah, held his fist still, mid-punch above Noah's face when he saw Terry coming with the knife pointed at them; he looked puzzled, and stood up slow. The other kid saw him, too, and let go of Francis's shirt. He dropped a cigarette, held his hands open palmed at both sides of his ribcage.

Terry kept his pace, sauntered an even gait, and bore down on the two of them, held each body and face in his mind at once, cued his arm, the knife, to any move they might make. But they stayed as they had been, still stuck, bewildered at him stomping toward them, no sign of halt or conciliation in his grip and the blade point. He stopped between Noah and Francis and kept his arm straight, elbow locked, swung the knife in wide circles like he turned a pirouette. Both the big kid and the other one took quick steps backward.

Alright, the biggest one said. Alright, cool out.

Back the goddamn fuck up, Terry said.

He said this as if ordering cattle to pen.

Just stop, the biggest one said.

You're being stupid, the other one said.

Terry looked hard at both of them, felt as sure and clearheaded as any moment he could remember before. The coming words were a nettle in his throat, there, but culled now, here on this green lawn, because of the knife, and the night, and Noah and Francis, the only two who stopped for him and called him theirs. Terry summoned them forth like a hungry ghost.

I will end your lives, right now, Terry said.

Francis drove fast in Noah's car, Terry in the passenger seat, Noah gone flat and drop-eyed in the back. Terry thought of the girl through the smoke, thought of the hips on the girl at the hearse, thought of holding the knife and speaking law, thought of the trembled lips on the big kid, cold sweat on the other's cheeks, thought how, from this point, things could not go back the other way. Trouble was waking, and soon, he would answer to it.

Are you fucking crazy? Francis said.

No, Terry said. I don't think so.

We're dead now.

Stop it.

I'm serious. Those cats aren't just big and fucking mean. They're ones to keep grudges.

Well.

So you bring a knife, they're going to want somebody to answer for that. All those people there, fuck man, all of them, makes it worse.

They can come and get me if they want. I'm not scared.

You should be.

Francis drove around through neighborhoods until he said his head was clear. They smoked a cheap cigar, cut down the middle with a razor blade and filled with dope and scrap tobacco. It took a long time to burn. By the end Terry's face and limbs felt slack, like pillow feathers, and he wondered if his innards were cotton, actually, not blood and organ, or if he was a robot, like from one of the movies they showed late at night on television.

Play that tape, Francis said.

What?

Your radio.

It's under his face.

Francis kept a hand on the wheel and leaned back and smacked Noah at the stomach with the other one.

Move bastard.

He jerked his arm, looked to the road to keep straight.

Hold the wheel, Francis said. He's using it like a fucking pillow.

Terry put a cigarette in his mouth, leaned over and took the wheel. The car had a lean, drifted left with the wheels straight. It took a moment for him to feel it out; the top of the wheel turned to the rearview kept the line. Francis twisted at the hips, and held his feet beside the pedals, reached back farther and gathered it up. He didn't take the wheel, but held the radio at his chest and pressed the button to play the tape. The heads dragged, then stopped. Francis gripped it on both ends and shook it like a change bank, or a present.

The batteries are dry, he said.

He put the radio to his lap. The car clipped a mailbox, broke it sideways into a yard. Francis didn't move his eyes. He said Shit, and kept driving. A few houses passed. He drifted to another yard and went head on against a thick postal beam. The metal letterbox on top cracked a jagged line on the windshield and twisted off the car to the road. Terry fingered the seatbelt at his waist.

Where are all these fucking mailboxes coming from? Francis said.

Noah's breath caught. He snorted loudly.

They're in the yards, Terry said.

I can't see, Francis said. Everything's dark.

He woke up in his clothes, shoes tied, gray wool socks bunched at his ankles. The house was quiet, night still, and he felt guilty, but couldn't figure why. He left his room, looked for his father in the kitchen and called for him in the hall.

The smoke peeled from his skin in the shower. He went to the kitchen and laid on the long wooden table beneath the tall windows, smoked on his back from the small brass pipe. The light came through the rising smoke and pressed warm against him; again, he slept, and when he woke up, his father stood beside the table, his trunk stretched funhouse slim in the window glare.

What are you doing son?

Terry looked to his feet. The light on the table was gone. He wore a towel.

Nothing, he said. I fell asleep.

Here? Benjamin Webber said.

Yes.

You smoking in here?

Me?

Terry, goddammit, yes you.

No, man.

Open a damn window, son.

5 9

I N THE late afternoon Terry pawned the dead man's coins for thirty dollars, and then he gave the money to Noah to put toward an ounce. He wore the wedding band, liked the way it felt when he turned it on his middle finger. He took it off, read a date cut in cursive script to the inside, fourth of June, 1934, and names, too; Howard Wilkins, Mozelle Small-good.

6 0

THEY TOOK Noah's car. Terry rode in the back. They pooled money for dope and a room.

The place was part of an old two-story house, bottom and top floors divided into three small apartments. Their door was red. The outside of the house was gray.

For three days in April the kids from Echota got their parents to rent houses at one block on the north end of the state's neon beach. They went around screaming and opening their chests; sometimes they went outside and lay down in the sun; sometimes they didn't notice the person sleeping beside them.

Noah's mother rented the place for them. He toothed the key in the lock, and when he turned it, the key went around loose and didn't click. He took it out and shook the brass knob, put a hand on the door and pushed it open. The lights were off, square window with blinds in the front room, dust clouded in light holed through the slits. There was a brown, sand colored couch against one wall, sink and counter on the other. Francis went to the bedroom. The mattress whined.

Noah came out to the front room with a joint, sat down on the rotten couch, Terry expectant and crosslegged on the floor.

Here, here, here, Noah said.

The joint looked like a plaster cast for a baby's arm.

That thing is terrible, Terry said.

Past the thin wall Francis snored low, even breaths.

Eventually a doorbell rang, but the place didn't have a doorbell. The lock didn't work, even.

Someone's at the door, Terry said. I'm hearing things, I think.

Noah stood up and wobbled, went over and opened the door on nothing. He came back and sat down again at the couch. Terry's mouth clenched, eyes jerked and his cheeks yanked with them.

I think something's wrong with the smoke, he said.

He heard bird wings, like playing cards shuffled and cut. Blood went up at his face and then left; he felt cold for some reason, and moved his ears for the first time.

Look at my ears, Terry said.

He moved them up and down. The sun cracked bright through the blinds. Outside the world caught fire.

Where are my spectacles? Noah said.

He rubbed his eyes.

You don't wear spectacles, Terry said.

I should.

Francis slept. Terry and Noah went out and started on the main road, passed houses painted mint and pale yellow, brown and white, salt peeled on the sides and stilted, raised high at balconies, kids burnt and dangling there, music a throb in the stirred air and salt light. They hunched for three blocks, and then they took stairs to the back room of the second level on a green house. Inside, it smelled old, and wet. Terry shook his arms to see if they were still there. Someone gave him a beer.

One kid tried to kiss a girl sat next to him. He leaned toward her. She didn't look at him, kept her face straight, and took a hand soft to his cheek and pushed him away. The kid smiled, head lolled forward, eyes jerked shut and then open. Terry stared at the kid's gold capped front teeth, suddenly his mouth was full of pennies; a dollar's worth, it looked. The kid went to kiss the girl again, didn't seem to remember what came before, even after the fourth time she pushed his face back.

Just take him somewhere, okay? she said.

She didn't look at anyone when she spoke. Noah got up anyway, and Terry did, too. Noah leaned down over the kid and put a hand on his shoulder like he gripped the end of a church pew.

Man, come outside, he said. I need to show you a good place to lay down. It's choice, if anything.

The kid nodded, seemed to like what he heard. He stood up, taller than both of them, and he wore a thin beard. Noah led him out of the front room and down the plank board stairs.

In the backyard Noah pointed him to the small opening at the base of the back wall, a door that led to the crawl space under the house. The kid crouched, lifted the cover and went feet first. The door fell behind. They stood and waited to see if he'd come out. Noah looped his hands over a clothesline at their backs and pulled, plastic cord stretched down at his weight. He picked an empty beer bottle near his feet, turned the nose down and threw it high over the house at the dark road in front of them. Terry fished the dead man's pills from his field jacket.

I don't know what they are, Terry said.

He rattled them in the plastic bottle, opaque, orange brown, and the cap white, label handwrote and faded. Noah took the bottle and studied the label a moment and then he uncapped the lid. He put one to his mouth and chewed, shook another and held it to him a fistful.

Take it, man, he said. It's fine. My uncle's a nurse.

Yeah?

He will be in two years. But he's got the uniform and everything.

The pill was shaped like a football. Terry palmed it, fat and thick in his hand. He studied the pill and then he threw it back. His mouth lacked spit. He bit hard, tasted chalk. Noah put the bottle into a pocket, and then he took it out again quickly and uncapped the lid, looked inside and shook the pills around. He pinched another one, thought for a breath, and then he ate it, lips grazed powder blue.

They took the stairs back up and stood in the kitchen. Some of the ones from the back room came out and milled around. The bony, dark-haired girl from the guesthouse in Echota was there. She came over and stood in front of him with another girl called Finley. Right above her bellybutton, moving up to her ribcage, was a thick straight line, rough and pink, like a zipper yanked out. Terry wanted to put his hands to it. Things in the room were looped and funny, like a stranger's family picture album, like church on television. She let the shirt drop, and took a sip from the red cup, ice beaded drops on the plastic, chewed teeth marks along the white lip.

I dig your wavelength, Terry said.

What? she said.

She put the cup to her mouth, gnawed at a spot already worked on.

Nothing, Terry said.

Noah mixed a glass of grain alcohol with pink instant lemonade powder. Terry drank it straight, and then Noah made another one, and Terry took that one up, too, and drank fast. His face started to beat warmly, hands, thighs, and then his groin went hot in the same way. The ground shifted beneath him. Noah's face dropped off. One of the girls grew ten feet to a terrible giant.

Terry's feet were light on the stairs going down, plank rail trembling beneath his right hand; he spit flowers in the yard, fell on the hood of a fast red car, felt his hands slide cool beside the air vent.

Terry woke beside the house, looked up at Noah's face and his stubby hand held down to him. He propped himself on his elbows.

What's all this about? Terry said.

His shirt was wet on the front. He thought maybe he was dead, or dreaming he was dead. He tried to stand but could not.

Deceased, Terry said.

He got to his knees, wobbled and fell back against the ground. He took Noah's hand and pulled himself up, looked then at his jeans, wet at the front, groin to thigh. He strained his head over one shoulder and looked at the backside of his jeans.

I might have pissed myself, he said.

Happens, Noah said.

Terry blinked at the night around him, thought he felt a bug crawl at his neck, and slapped it with a hard swat. He looked at his hand; nothing. He shook it, then. He smacked his lips and it made a noise like tape peeled back from cardboard.

Where's that red door? Terry said.

He stood still for a moment. Noah dusted grass from his shoulders and pointed to the street at his back.

Terry walked fast, and thought it must be morning, the air wet and pregnant, but it was still night.

He passed another white house with the lights up. In the front yard three men stood at the back of a silver car like moviegoers. Another lay like a sunbather in the grass, lit pink in the taillights, feet out front, propped up to his elbows. Terry didn't want to know what it was they were doing. He smelled menace, felt some ancient fight playing out. He kept his face down, tried not to look, but he couldn't stop his eyes from turning up.

Someone said, Hello!

Terry lifted his face, spoke loud to the night dark.

Hello! he said. How are you!

He walked a little faster, crossed his arms jacket tight over his chest.

Two of them came out of the dark and took each of his arms at the bicep. It was not a hard grip. They turned him around, and he walked with them.

Okay, he said. Okay, okay, okay.

Terry's feet turned pink in the headlights. He studied the man laid there, a boy, really, who looked Terry's age, or maybe a little older, eyes wet, but not from crying. Terry took in the rest; all of them boys, he saw, faces twisted brown liquor drunk. One of them explained that the boy on the ground was a good friend of all of theirs, but he'd stolen a hundred dollars from one of them.

I did, the boy on the ground said.

He leaned to one arm and raised the other one.

I did do it, he said. I stole. That money and all what.

We don't know what to do about it, one of them said.

Oh, I don't care, the boy at the ground said. Just get on with it. All of you tiny shitcakes.

We thought maybe we should hit him with sticks, another one said.

Terry saw, then, that all of them were holding large branches torn from a bush or tree.

Those aren't sticks, Terry said.

They didn't seem to hear him.

That's fine, the one on the ground said. Hit me with sticks and whatall. The branches. Whatever the shit they are.

I think that's a good idea, Terry said.

He didn't realize that he'd started to cry; more than anything else, he wished to get away from these four. Terry turned to leave and one of them took his arm again, then bent down to the ground, picked up a branch and held it to him.

What? Terry said.

Terry looked at the one on the ground; he was set on seeing this through. Terry waited, and the others started with the branches, and then the rush of cut air took him, white trails from the branches whimpered in the dark. He raised the branch and brought it down against one of the kid's shoulders. He felt scared, but good at the same time. He kept swinging, felt each tiny moment of the world turned solid and clear in the sharp whack of wood against bone. The one on the ground clutched his gut, and they stopped hitting him, all of them gripping split branches. The one on the ground raised himself to an elbow and spit, wiped his mouth at both corners with his sleeve.

Terry heard his heart in his ears and ribs when he stumbled away from them. He pushed open the red door; dark inside the room, Noah splayed on the couch, red metal flashlight on the floor beside him like a stowed rifle. Terry went over and took it up and shined it down on his face. Noah had dark, elegant and swooping eyebrows drawn over his real ones with a deep black marker, and a curled mustache over his top lip. He looked like a matador. Terry told him so, even though Noah was sleeping, and patted his head, hair dark wet and cold, breath low and patient through his nose. He turned off the flashlight and put it back on the floor and then he went to the corner beside the couch and sat down, pulled his knees high to his chest.

6 1

THE SAND was warm around the house stilts. Terry's eyes hurt. They walked on the side of the road and stopped in front of a house painted brown and orange. Noah hustled up the stairs to the deck, touched a girl on the back, close to her shoulder blades. She turned around and put her arms over his shoulders. She smiled, had tall shoulders and red skin, wore swimming goggles with blue lenses and a white rubber strap banded at the crown of her head. Noah pointed down to Francis and Terry, barefoot in the sand, and they squinted up to her like they were seeing a monument for the first time. She waved, and they waved back.

Who's that? Terry said.

He forgot, with the grain alcohol, the night before, that he'd studied her stomach, the pale scar above her navel.

Merriam something or other, Francis said. She has a great ass.

She faced them, and Terry couldn't see.

I can't see her ass, he said.

The house was like the place before, one large and bare space at the front, a pair of bunkrooms on back, walls colored clay and shale. A disco ball hung from a twisted clothes hanger jammed at the ceiling. Pieces of particleboard fell to a small pile near the center of the room, and people stepped over it, and tapped the disco ball when they passed beneath.

In the bathroom a girl sat on the toilet with the lid turned down, vanity mirror at her lap. She hunched over it, rounded her spine, back heaving when she drew in through her one nostril and then the other. She put her fingers to her mouth, traced her gums and teeth with the tips, the motion shaped a dance in the mirror above the sink. Terry stood back against the door. There were four people in the bathroom. They used a cut-off purple straw. He didn't know what it would do shot up his nose to his brain, but he put his face on the mirror, anyway, held his left nostril closed with his thumb and sucked in. For a moment, nothing, but then whatever he nosed spread inside him, felt like cough syrup did when he drank mouthfuls, felt like the sound of a car running too high in a low gear, pistons burning. He put his shoulders and the small of his back against the wall, couldn't swallow, felt lead in his teeth, sulfur on his tongue.

Terry left the bathroom and went to one of the bedrooms. Francis got the cigarette near his mouth, and then the door opened and squared him on the back. He fell down, cigarette flown to a clothes pile. A pink shirt on top started to smolder, and then more pieces caught, and everyone around him stood up and moved fast from the room. Noah and Francis were gone then, screeching yells from the yard batted the windows. Terry sat a moment, leaned his head to one side and watched the pile catch. He meant to see them burn, take the room and then the house, but he stood up when the smoke got thick and hazed in the room, stepped over to the fire and stomped at it. His right pants leg caught, burned some on the cuff. He punched it out, turned back to work on the mound, hopped boot heels until the clothes did not weep. Most were charred on top, blacked patches and smelling like cold weather. Terry sat back down on the bed and started a cigarette. He smoked slow, stayed a moment to make sure the pile did not catch again; he did not understand police were in the front yard, gathering handfuls of kids from the house, smell of billy club and handcuff in the air, officers working like those who tended bar, like deacons, cobblers or stonemasons.

Terry left the house at the back stairs and ran west though the yards. He made back to the main road, slowed his gallop to a careful walk, like stepping over graves.

Merriam was standing in the side yard of another house. The ones swarmed there were screaming on the ricket porch and in the yard. She leaned on a small red truck parked a drunk slant, and smoked a long, white filter cigarette, looking like a woman in the old movies on television, and he wondered if she ever wore a tiara, some diamond beaded headband. Behind him the police took apart the house, a storm of navy and flashlight, scattering all of them with the weight of gold badges and nightsticks. Merriam didn't turn when he came up, didn't say anything. Terry stood close to her. He didn't know why, had never thought to do such a thing, but he pressed his waist into hers, nudged her feet with his in the sand-choked grass.

I saw you back there, Terry said. I can't remember when that was. Today, I think.

Yesterday afternoon. Last night.

Francis said your ass is bionic.

That's right.

And before, I saw you, too.

Right.

You were leaning on that piano.

It was a nice one. Don't turn around.

Terry was confused for a moment. Merriam dropped the cigarette at his feet and stood close to his chest, turned her face on his.

Don't do anything yet, Merriam said.

She spoke close to his mouth, her breath warm, night wet.

Listen, she said. They took a left just back there, and they're going to come around this way.

She bumped her head in the opposite direction. Terry gripped her on the wrist and thought to run, but she took his wrist with her other hand, and stopped him.

If you do that, she said, it will look very bad. In five seconds they will be here. They'll let the sirens go, and the world will light up like a fucking atom bomb.

The police cars stormed the lot and the sirens wailed, the late dark gone loud and blue and red and white and flashing like some county fair. Merriam pulled him to her chest, said something close to his ear he couldn't make, and then she kissed him hard, and he followed her mouth; this moment stretched for some time. She pulled back and turned around quickly in the sand and led him on the road past the wide backs and shoulders of

the police, the lit faces of startled kids, some at a sprint, some thrown to
the ground. All of it happened in the sudden manner of a winter storm.

Soon they knocked at the red door and went inside. Merriam sat down in
one corner near the window, and ground her teeth. It sounded like green
wood snapping. Terry pulled the blue snow hat down to cover his ears,
and then he went over to her and took her hand and pulled her up.

What are we doing? she said.

Don't be silly, Terry said.

He didn't know what to do. He took a pale pink sheet from one of the
beds, and a small chair from the corner, stuffed one end of the spread into
a drawer and draped the other over the chair back, and then he sat crosslegged underneath it.

It's a tent, Merriam said.

She sat beside him. He took a lighter from one pocket, flame lit the
blanket underneath.

A teepee, actually, he said.

You want to tell me something? she said.

I would, he said.

The words went sour and to a mash in his throat, and he couldn't make
any sense of them. Merriam took his hands and held them at her lap. He
didn't want her to look at them, didn't want her to see the lines cut there.
He leaned over fast and kissed her on the mouth. They stayed a moment,
and then she pulled away, reached up, yanked the spread down in ruins.

He stood up when she left the house and draped the spread over his shoulders like a cape. He went into the front room and paced, looked a dog at
the gate of a yard fence. He sat down in one corner for what seemed a
long time, and he tried to sleep, but could not.

The next morning Noah kicked his leg. Terry blinked, slapped both
cheeks to shake his head. Francis slept on the floor. The rest of them were
gone. The room smelled sharp and desperate.

Get up bastard, Noah said.

Alright, goddammit, Terry said.

Noah thumped Francis at the ear. Francis rubbed his eyes and sat up
and propped his arms behind.

Is it time? he said.

Yeah, Noah said.

Is there work? Terry said. Are we farming?

They got stoned and drove to a long white rectangle church built high on stilts. It was Easter; the preacher threw God at them, knocked handfuls down between the pews.

ON THE Monday and Tuesday after Easter he stayed home from school. He sat in the backyard on the grass and it was quiet. But on Wednesday it turned cool, and he went back to class, and then later the hearse idled in front of the house.

Carly sat in front. Louden was her boyfriend. He opened the small window between the front and back. Terry sat in the rear seat, as wide and long as a bench in the bus station. They passed a joint. Ashes tipped at the front, and Carly dusted them off. Terry thought about her hips, wished to put his hands there. He thought about her bare stomach and the brass snap on her jeans, thought about ghosts in the wide casket space over his shoulders, how many cries the hearse knew. He felt the road change and the cold past the open windows, and the red metal of the hearse run fast through the night. Louden pulled into the driveway and cut the engine, pistons sputtering, then slowed, belts smacked loose on the metal. Terry saw then it was very dark outside.

The band practiced in a cinder block, white painted house with a septic tank at one side, shaped round like an ornament for a Christmas tree. There was a steep drop down to a parking lot behind. The spaces drawn at the lot below were faded, blacktop split by weeds. There were two shops built at the back of the lot; dance hall, paint store, windows boarded with knotted shanks of pine. They got out of the hearse and walked up to the house. Carly pecked at gravel with a shoe toe, and then she opened the door.

In the front room people sat on a long yellow couch and in lawn chairs and on the floor. There was a hole in the floor, near the middle of the room. One of them finished a cigarette and thumped it there; it kept burning, put arms of smoke in the room, and then someone threw another one to the pit. Cold air shot through and drafted the room. Some people's breath fogged. Louden went over and looked down into the pit. Carly and Terry stood back some, like they expected a fireball to leap out.

That's a fire waiting, Louden said.

One of the kids nodded.

It'd help, Louden said. This cold damn place.

He opened the door on a woodstove in one corner, poked coals with a fire-blacked hanger, balled a section of newspaper from the floor and put a match on it. The paper caught, and then he tossed it into the stove. The flame hissed and rose. Louden shut the door and fixed the latch, flame jumping behind a jagged fist-size hole in the stovepipe. There was a record player at one side of the stove, two cabinet speakers at either side. The music from the speakers was loud and fast, garbled like a fistfight. There was a glass pipe, a spoon they called it, colored blue and green and orange, passed to all of them, the head a deep bowl. There were many wallets with long chains attached, and a mannequin in one corner missing both legs and one arm.

Isaac Calendar played a beat Strat knockoff, stickers pasted to the neck and body of the guitar over pieces knocked out. He had a large silver paper clip stuck through his left earlobe. He sat the guitar flat on his lap and rested a beer on top. The tattoo artist set up a drum kit. It was small; bass, tom, snare, brass metal crash, white tape patched crosses on top.

LOUDEN LIVED in a house connected to four others, skinny and high, each one painted grade school crayon; blue, purple, pink, and yellow. The hearse was parked in the drive, back end facing the road, and there was a brown Firebird missing wheels and set on cinder blocks. Louden asked if he could play a bass guitar, and he couldn't, even a little, but he thought maybe he listened to enough records. The bass player, for some reason, had just stopped showing up.

We need one, Louden said. It doesn't matter if you're good or not.

Alright, Terry said.

Louden scooped a wooden head driver from the yard. He focused, still, and swung the club. He cut a square of grass. The clod jumped a few feet, then fell back down and broke apart when it hit.

You just stand there is all, Louden said.

He stuck his boot at the club hole.

I should have been a goddamn golfer, he said. A real pro. A jock. A looper.

They went up the front stoop to the tattoo artist's house and pushed a jagged screen door to go inside. The same people from before sat in the front room, on the yellow couch, smoking cigarettes and drinking beer from blue and silver aluminum cans. Terry sat down between two of them. Louden lapped the length of the room and pulled a smoke, exhaled a stream that trailed behind. He stopped halfway on the second lap and lifted a guitar high at the neck, black lacquer, sharp pointed ears. He plugged the cable to a small amp.

Can you hold down a string? Isaac said.

Yeah, Terry said. I think so.

He wasn't sure at all. Isaac got up and went over to some tangled cables. The drums sat stacked in the corner, apple red bass leaned to the wall beside the kit. Terry went over and put a hand to the fat neck, touched the strings with the underside of a thumb, thick wound gray metal, like power lines. He picked it up, draped it to his right shoulder.

Isaac Calendar fixed small pieces of masking tape at the frets, etched letters there in black pen. One named John Quality sat at the drums. Isaac tuned his guitar and looked at Terry standing in the middle of the room, bass at his shoulder like a rifle turned over. He slung the guitar to his back, neck down, and walked over to pick up a cable head. He jammed it to a hole near the foot of the bass, and then passed Terry a string pick, big as a half dollar. Terry pressed the top string at the first fret with his left index finger, did the same at the third fret and then the fifth. The amps hummed, the room filled with blind static. The singer, one called Conrad Frankenstein, held a microphone in one hand, black cable wrapped on both, hands like a boxer's, like Christ's. The drums, and then the guitar went loud; Conrad Frankenstein delirious at a scream. Terry watched Isaac and Louden, and he started to get the hang of how things worked. He felt the drums on his back. He felt monsters in his chest.

Merriam sat on one end of the yellow couch. He hadn't seen her come inside, didn't consider, even, that she'd come to such a place. After a while Terry's fingers bled. He yanked the plug and propped the bass to one amp and sat on the floor next to her. Isaac and Louden, John Quality and Conrad Frankenstein kept going, two songs, then four more. Merriam handed down a joint, leaned at Terry's ear and spoke muffled. He shook his head and held up both hands, and she bent down again, mouth against his ear, and she kept it there.

Terry turned on the light in the bathroom and locked the door, heard the band through the walls, an old scream, cymbal crashed brass sharp, and he thought about Merriam, her lips against his ear. He washed his hands and dried them on a yellow hand towel. The knob rattled loose and twisted on the door.

Someone's in here, he said.

Merriam closed the door behind her and leaned against it, hair light brown and limp at her shoulders. Her t-shirt was green, and read HUGS, NOT DRUGS.

That lock doesn't work, Merriam said.

She pulled the shirt up over her head and dropped it on the floor, hummed a song he didn't know. He thought about Alice Washington, how she made her voice very big while singing. He thought about how he'd never seen a girl just take her shirt off like that.

Come here, she said.

She hummed again. Terry got an erection, put his hands to it and pressed it down, drew his hips in and kept his hands there.

I don't know if I'm ready for that just yet, he said.

He stumbled at the lip of the bathtub and almost fell back. Merriam put her hands on his shoulders and turned him around, and then she pushed him back against the door.

You ever been with a girl like this?

No.

He thought of Alice Washington, her finger in his mouth.

Lay down, she said.

He did. She put a leg on either side of him, sat down and pressed herself against his chest.

You don't have to do anything, she said.

He felt her hand undoing his belt, then his zipper.

Nothing?

Just lay there, she said.

He was inside her, then, and she rocked on top of him, eyes down at his face, then back up. She got his hands at the wrists.

You can put them right here, she said.

She led his hands to where her thighs met her stomach.

Like this?

He closed his eyes, but did not want to; Alice Washington pointing at the great owl; Alice Washington at the movies; Alice Washington kissing his neck; Alice Washington beneath the Indian head penny bar sign; Alice Washington through the station wagon's back glass; Alice Washington turned over; Alice Washington held with a seatbelt; Alice Washington gone ash; he was crying; Merriam was moving faster.

O N FRIDAY Terry went to Louden's house after dark. Louden
said the first one should hurt. They used plastic black ink pens.
It was only small letters, five to spell his name. Louden boiled water on
the stove and held the razor blade with metal tongs in the moving water.
Terry rolled his sleeve and pulled it tight over his right shoulder. His
hands tingled. He felt the blood warm down over his bicep and forearm.
He stood on a spread newspaper. The headline read RAIN, RAIN, GO AWAY.
The blood ran off his fingers and dropped at the newspaper. Louden
dabbed the letters with a paper napkin. Terry winced, and the room wobbled dizzy and cold. Louden looked at him hard, lit a cigarette, blew
smoke.

Don't move, he said.

He broke the ink shaft with two hands, and held the split plastic on top
of the razor cuts. He dropped the tube against the newspaper and
smeared his hands over the letters and held them there. Terry's arm was
dark blue, and some red, and throbbed at his heartbeat. He held it
straight out and Louden covered his bicep with plastic wrap and pulled it
tight.

Terry was crying.

South Carolina's first cash crop was indigo, Louden said. Blue ink.

He mashed out the cigarette on the floor, and then he lit another, blew
smoke at the side of his mouth. Terry stomped his foot hard. Louden
smiled.

Awhile now, he said.

His arm throbbed. He touched the clear tape wrapped bandage and stared as they passed streetlamps. They got stoned off pot that tasted charcoal. He went through half a pack. They drove the same loop four times through one of the old neighborhoods. The dope made him feel mean, and tall, and blank, and his arm burned, and he wanted to tear it off, drop it from the window.

The front yard of the old wood finished two-story was wet. There was a long porch on the front and kids leaned at the rail and against the wall and sat in lawn chairs. In the front room there was a gas fireplace with fake logs tossed orange and white, and some sat on a couch, and some on the floor around a coffee table littered with bottles and cans. There were ashes on the floor and in the air. In the backyard a fire burned, and people stood around in small knots on the dark grass. Terry and Louden went and stood by Francis. He told them Noah was at home and asleep.

I cut him, Louden said.

Francis wore the blue mesh baseball hat. He pulled up the sleeve and looked on the bandage. He squinched his eyes, dropped the sleeve back.

What's that mean?

I don't know, Terry said. It's my name.

Did it hurt?

Yeah.

Bad?

Real bad.

Did you cry?

Some.

I would have.

They threw dented cans in the fire. Francis tossed a handful of dirt. The clouds ticked fast over the moon, blue frame, white haze.

Louden kept his eyes fixed on the road. He took a cigarette from behind his ear and put it to his mouth. He rolled down the window and blew smoke. Terry watched him drive with his sure and crunched face. There was madness inside Louden; his heart, fist and bone, a hundred screams. Terry's hands and the blue word on his bicep burned. Some blood came from beneath the tape on his arm. He balled his shirt at the bottom and wiped it.

My old man, Louden said. That fucker, when I was twelve, he got a railroad spike in his temple. He worked there, I mean, for the railroad, on the tracks, fixing things that went wrong, and once he slipped on those rocks, you know the ones that are always on railroad tracks, those slick fat ones that are all jammed up together? He slipped on those. You'd think there'd be a train or something. But no. He slipped. It took a small piece out. The skull, I mean. It fucked up his head some, made him mean, mostly, but also he can't clean himself anymore. Not like he shits himself, just that he doesn't have any sense of personal hygiene, like the idea of brushing your teeth, or washing yourself, doesn't mean anything to him. Like even after people told him, he didn't do anything, because he couldn't, like his brain had lost that one single part. Everything else, besides being a fucking asshole, I mean. That was mostly there already, everything else was fine, normal. Not at all out of the ordinary. The smell of this man, though, I'm telling you, is incredible.

65

THEY PILED amps and cords and guitars and drums back of the hearse and drove it over to the American Legion a few hours before the show started. It was their first one. He rode with Louden and John Quality and Isaac Calendar and Carly and a girl named Roxanne. She wore fire engine red lipstick, and her black t-shirt read CRIB DEATH.

The building was in the woods out past the county airport. There were pictures on the walls of old men sitting at tables in the same building. They had small heads, and big glasses, wore army or navy or marine or air force hats, and pins and ribbons and wings at their shirts.

Roxanne Crib Death unhinged one of the pictures and laid it on the table. She spilled two blue pills on the glass and crushed them with the bottom of a beer bottle. She put her nose to the old men's faces past the glass and the powder. Terry went down on it next. He came up fast, and tried to move his eyes far back in his head. He wiped his nose and sniffed.

He went back over to the wall and looked at the pictures some more and took out a cigarette. He patted his chest. One could do a lot with pilot's wings. He thought about his grandfather, how he was dead.

The place filled up with smoke and bodies, the smell of wet mouths, punk kids from Echota and the spent towns nearby. He wasn't ready to play in front of people, not even a little. Isaac said he was fine. If he fucked up no one would hear anyway.

He meant to come down a little. He walked laps at the room. He smoked a joint with Isaac and Roxanne Crib Death under the pictures of old men. The two of them left, and Terry stayed looking at the pictures. The cigarettes piled at his feet.

He took most of the skin from the index finger on his right hand by the fifth song. He drug it over and over against the strings on a down pick. The tips of every one save the pinky on his left bled. Louden jumped off the stage on the eighth song, and then he saw him at the small crowd up front, shouldered through a swarm that crashed one another. He moved through the bodies. He parted them.

66

MONDAY HE opened the first stall door at the bathroom on the math hall. There was a cinder block dropped in the toilet. He went to the next stall, locked the door and put his back to it. He got a cigarette. He kept it at his mouth, and pissed the same time, and then a hard knock at the door, and he let the cigarette fall from his mouth to the toilet. He fanned the smoke, and brought a foot to the silver knob and flushed. He turned and opened the door.

Merrill stood arms crossed over his chest. He played on the team, sometimes midfield, mostly up front. Terry nodded at him, and started to walk past.

I thought you were a teacher, he said.

He went to the sink and turned the water, pressed the box holding the pink soap, and washed his hands. Merrill stood behind.

I already know what you're going to say, Terry said.

He didn't know. He pressed for more soap, worked it into his fingers.

She's his girlfriend, Merrill said.

She can think for herself, Terry said.

He got a brown paper towel and dried his hands. Merrill leaned against the back wall. He stretched his head toward the bathroom door.

You got an extra?

Terry unzipped the back pocket on his knapsack and took out a cigarette.

First stall's got a cinder block in the toilet, Terry said.

Merrill went to the back. The smoke curled one side of the stall. The toilet flushed loud, violent, and Merrill fumbled with the door and stepped out and wobbled some. He looked in the mirror at the other sink and ran water at his hands.

You three got a bad deal, Merrill said. Shouldn't have kicked you off.

I don't care anything about that coach or that team. You can all fuck off for all I care.

Merrill shook his head slow.

Just look out is all I'm saying.

His jaw hurt. He thought about pulling teeth, counting them.

Benjamin Webber and the dog came inside the house damp from the grass and the rain stood puddles. The dog was gray and white haired, spotted places on the back legs with mange, and its ribs bared some. It came over and stood in front.

It's your dog, his father said.

Terry leaned and put a hand beneath its jaw and rubbed there. The dog panted a gum red open mouth.

It doesn't have any teeth, he said.

Doesn't matter. It's been going on sticks, tearing them to shit all afternoon.

He squatted deep at his heels and looked the dog in the face. It huffed. His father got the back leg and rubbed a humped spot in the fur.

He's got a damn BB in his leg, he said.

Terry felt the hump, metal buried, and skin grown over. He father loosed the back leg and the dog stayed and tilted its head one side and looked on the yard.

Somebody shot him?

I guess. He doesn't give a shit.

Is it old?

I don't think so. It's been hanging around the dumpster at work.

Well where's the damn teeth?

Maybe they fell out.

The dog smiled bare gummed at him and shook its heavy gray tail.

A dog doesn't need teeth to be a dog.

Terry turned to leave the kitchen and the dog followed him.

H E KNOCKED her front door, and then she came out and stood in front of him. She looked down at the dog. It huffed.

Whose dog? she said.

Mine.

It's a mutt.

You shut up.

They were quiet for a while. The dog nosed the porch, lay down a few feet away and put its head at its front feet.

Wayne, she said.

Who?

My man.

Oh.

He's going to find you. I'm sorry.

What's that mean?

It means I'm sorry.

Does me no fucking good.

He's mean.

I know he's mean.

He's big.

Alright.

I mean it. I had to tell him. I was scared. He came at me, stood me against the wall in my room.

Kick his balls.

He said he's going to get you for kissing on me.

You were kissing on me.

That doesn't matter.

I know.

You should make plans.

How should we end this?

You pick.

She closed the door. He stood and looked at it awhile. He called the dog over. He thought of nuclear warheads, just below the dirt, winter drowned plains.

68

HIS FATHER showed him the paper next day, thumbed a picture from the front page of a tree through a house. They fell in the storm, and lines broke, and the wind touched sixty. A man two miles past the city limit stayed out in the wind and pulled clothes from a line, and part of his roof broke off. He kept, but then he took a two-by-four into his head, above the left ear, and it lodged and almost touched his brain, and then a doctor pulled it out and wrapped bandages over the hole.

A few days he thought about her, and his head fumed. He was confused. He scribbled a note, asked her to meet him at a silo he knew. He left it on her front step.

He shut the dog in the house, and walked six miles outside of town.

The silo was bullet gray and rust sealed, at the end of a dirt road, fell corn on both sides. A small white house stood dark against the trees in back of the field, and no cars were out front. He walked inside and saw slits in the domed roof of the silo, light coming through onto the curved walls behind him. He sat in the dirt, and stared at the door panel. He waited for it to open.

He heard her feet soft, and the car door pushed shut, and then she stood in the doorway and looked down on him. The light was strong at her back, and it pinned his eyes.

Would you shut the door, please? he said.

I don't want to, she said.

He stood up, and reached behind her and pulled the door closed. He turned and faced her. He couldn't make out her face so well in the dark. He stared hard, and he tried to see something there in her face. He didn't know what. He kissed her blind, or she kissed him. He was confused as to who started it.

He's going to find you, she said.

He shook his head.

I'm sorry.

You've said that already, he said. Could we just stop, please? You're like a fucking baby. You and all the rest.

Her face clinched some.

See? he said. Go back to the fucking baby house.

He pointed at the door. She looked at him hard.

What? he said.

He pointed to the door again, took her by one arm and pushed her toward it.

Get out of here, he said.

She stumbled when he pushed her again.

There's nothing to say, he said. Go the fuck home.

He sat down against the wall at his back and put his eyes on the dirt. She stepped over the bottom of the doorframe.

Shut the goddamn door, he said.

She did. It was late afternoon, the light had moved up the front wall of the silo, back toward the bent roof. It was almost gone.

MERRILL CAME by the shed in Noah's backyard. He wanted some hash. Since Noah and Francis and Terry didn't have practice anymore they spent most time in the shed after school. Francis took the lawnmower and almost everything else out, the empty red plastic gasoline canister, the round-headed shovel, the half-full bag of manure, the green metal rake, the orange extension cord, stored all of it in the space between the rear of the shed and the wire fence. He found a small metal trashcan behind the shed and brought it inside, moved it close to one of the slot windows. He built a small fire in the trashcan with broken sticks, brown leaves and lighter fluid, torn pieces of brown paper grocery bag. He piled more broken sticks at his feet and he leaned over the fire, small and orange against his forehead and his nose, and he dropped small pieces of stick to the fire, and they cracked in the fire and sent small sparks up to the top of the shed.

Merrill was quiet. He stood across from Francis and looked down at the flames and the smoke pulled by the high cold at the open window. He kept both hands inside his pockets. He didn't smoke cigarettes.

Noah twisted the hash up with some pot and tobacco, lit one end and put his eyes on the paper and watched the red ash skulk toward him when he pulled. He coughed. He put a hand against the shed door.

That's his girlfriend, Merrill said. You need to understand that.

Terry nodded. Merrill was pale in the floodlight.

I understand that.

I don't think you do. You can't talk to her like you did.

His eyes and voice were quiet, and dark. Terry went to look him in the face, but he couldn't. Merrill knew things that scared most people. That sort of peace scared Terry.

It's not right, Merrill said. What you did. Not even a little.

He lit a cigarette and handed it to Terry, and he got another and put it to his mouth.

Can't talk to anyone like that, Merrill said. You talk at me like that, I'll break your goddamn face.

Terry pulled at the hash.

There are things there you don't want, Merrill said. I'm saying that now. Now and here.

7 0

H E CAME alone and parked his car a street over. He pushed out through trees and made across the backyard of the house west of Merriam's. There were toys tossed in the grass; a bike, plastic shovels, a bucket. All the lights in the house were shut off. In one small tree children's shoes hung like ornaments, laces tied in the branches. There were shin-deep holes in the yard. He stumbled at one.

Wayne was there. Terry waited an hour and smoked, and ran it through in his head.

He jumped and got a hand to the top of the fence, and he held, got the other one, and pulled himself at the arms.

He came down feet and hands beside the pool, and the water was lit space blue and filled with old leaves. Everyone there stood in circles, fisted drinks and cigarettes, and smoke held past their heads in the floodlight.

He leaned against the fence for a moment and lit another cigarette. His mouth tasted like chalk. He heard voices inside the house.

He sat on the edge of the pool and put his shoes and jeans down in the neon water. He leaned back on his elbows.

Wayne's goons got him first. They grabbed him by the back of his jacket and pulled him up, stood in a jagged circle around him. They had the voices of birds. His eyes wobbled. He stopped on Mickel Really. His lips were fat, full of stitches. Terry smiled and scratched his nose.

Wayne pushed through the goons and stood in front of him. Terry's head butted Wayne's chin. They stood still a few moments. Terry lit a cigarette. Wayne turned and looked over one shoulder. Merriam stood against one of the tall glass back doors just outside their circle.

She's my girlfriend, Wayne said. I won't let you mess with that.

Terry looked at her.

This is what you want? he said.

Merriam stayed still, arms crossed. He smiled again and spit. He took another drag and turned back to Wayne.

Go on and have your baby party then, he said.

He sniffed quick, looked at Wayne again and waited.

Wayne's fist was warm, the punch dull at his mouth. Terry wobbled but then straightened up and touched his jaw. Wayne put a finger against his chest.

I won't stop next time I see you, he said.

He stood dazed a few moments, shook his head until it cleared.

Wayne took Merriam by the arm and went into the house. His goons fell in a few steps behind.

His mouth beat in a throb. He touched his lips and his fingers came back red. He spit blood, tongued a loose canine on the bottom.

He worked it out with two fingers. He threw it to the deep end.

He walked alleys downtown. He cursed, spit more blood.

He went fast on the sidewalk, the block between Irby and Northridge, and his hands jammed at his pockets.

The hearse rumbled, and it idled slow beside him. The window rolled down. Louden leaned over the passenger seat. Terry spit, opened the door and got inside.

Louden pulled back into the street. He gave Terry a beer. Terry washed a few swallows around in his mouth and spit it from the window and gave the bottle back.

He did that to you? Louden said.

Terry nodded.

I'm going away, Terry said.

Where? Louden said.

Terry looked around for the water tower in the west. He found it and pointed toward it.

That way, Terry said.

Louden drove and pulled hard on a cigarette, studied houses and trees gone past.

I saw that asshole shoot a crow once with a shotgun, Louden said. He winged it, watched it twitch on the ground. He stood over it and laughed, kicked it some. Just left it there not even dead.

Could you just drop me at my house, man? Terry said.

You need to clean Wayne up some.

What?

If you're leaving.

I am leaving.

Well then.

They waited a few houses down. The light started to come up. Louden stepped out and walked fast and his boots cracked gravel in the drive and Terry got out and it was cold and he stayed still a moment, and then he got a run and caught up. Louden kept his pace, sure and even.

They went up to the porch and knocked at the front door. Wayne's father came out on the steps and looked them over.

What, then?

We need to talk to Wayne, Louden said.

He studied them stern and unsure.

What do you need him for?

We got business, Louden said.

What kind?

Your boy busted my friend's mouth.

He did?

Yeah. Go and get him.

Louden pointed past his shoulder.

Go.

Who are you?

That's not important.

Do you know Wayne?

Get back there and get him.

Wayne's father crossed his arms on his chest. He looked at them some more.

You're serious?

Damn right.

He chuckled some.

I don't think you two and Wayne need to talk right now, he said.

Go and get him old man, Louden said.

Wayne's father looked jarred, knocked back with those words, the stone rage in Louden's face.

I'm not kidding a single bit, Louden said. Go. Right now.

Wayne shouldered past his father in the doorway and came onto the porch with the sleep still on his face.

What are you doing here? he said.

He blinked hard. Terry stepped up toward him.

I just wanted to talk, Terry said.

He held his hands up.

We don't have anything to talk about, Wayne said. This was done last night.

Wayne pointed to the dirt road leading away from his house and the sun still breaking low.

Get out of here, he said.

Terry rubbed his jaw, shook his head and smirked.

Leave, he said.

Man, Terry said. You're a fucking asshole.

I'm an asshole? he said.

Terry's face pinched; he bore his teeth and took a step. Wayne's father put an arm between them. Louden pulled it down. Wayne pushed Terry hard, and he fell over the steps onto his back. Wayne jumped down. His father shook from Louden and hopped down by Wayne. Louden got him at the back fast, bunched his collar and put him down a thud.

Terry felt some madness in his chest. He put a leg up and caught Wayne in the gut. He turned on his knees and got on top of him. He held his shirt at the front, and beat on his face, and then Wayne was limp, and his eyes watered, and he coughed some blood.

Louden pulled him off. They left Wayne and his father blind in the yard.

He had busted his right hand on Wayne's face. Louden took a few scratches at both arms. Terry's bottom lip bled. Louden shook his head in the hearse. He didn't slow for the tracks, and the hearse jumped, and dipped hard past the hump.

Dumb fucking old man acting like that, he said. He deserved that shit. You need to know that. Doesn't matter what anyone says.

Louden pulled away and didn't say much. Terry went fast to his room and stuffed his knapsack. He stopped in his father's room. Benjamin Webber was on a second week of some overtime at the plant. Terry went to the closet, reached high at the shelf and got down a shoebox. He opened it, counted four hundred dollars in twenties and tens, and then he put the box back. He put the dog in his room, left cereal and water at separate bowls, and he rubbed its head a moment, and the tail knocked fast, and the dog panted, and some spit ran from its mouth. Terry pointed to the water. He spoke to the dog.

See? he said. You need to drink that.

The dog stayed, kept beating its tail on the floor.

Dammit, Terry said. Like this.

Terry went over to the bowls and put his head down and lapped.

Terry wiped his nose in the car, hands dried blood and dirt. He drove from the neighborhood under the crooked oaks.

7 1

THE ONRAMP wound a fast circle, and gravity pulled him to one side and then the other, and he felt like a racecar driver, or a cavalry horse; the heads of new grass nodded on both shoulders when he passed.

The road was chipped in places, yellow and white lined, and on both sides there were the trees, the neon billboards, and the houses, and the frayed tire scrap left on the shoulder, and three pairs of tennis shoes, yellow ones, just stepped from.

E CROSSED mountains. He crossed the continental divide.

73

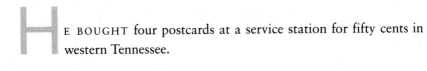 E BOUGHT four postcards at a service station for fifty cents in western Tennessee.

HE DREAMT a day, and got lost, drove eight hours north, and then he crossed the border to Indiana. He didn't know how he'd gotten there, but he felt good, anyway, the blunder like a gift.

The highway was iced and ran flat through cornfields and the air smelled of cow, damp earth and old leaves. He stopped for gas, and an old man handed him a glossed brochure, and he took it, and then he got in the car and studied it. He took the state highway ten miles to Fairmount, and then he drove through the old downtown, and houses turned into shops that sold pictures of the dead actor born there, and a record store kept a picture of him in the window, and then there was a diner named for him, and then the house of his birth. Terry went past the city limits, followed a map on the brochure. He stood at the grave, and his hands went red, and then he got back into the car and followed the pamphlet some more to the house of the actor's grandparents. The actor was a boy there. Terry stopped the car in the drive and cut the engine. The house was white and peeling, and the cold wind pushed through the bare trees on both sides. Terry got out of the car and went up to the front end and sat on the hood. He crossed his legs at the ankles, cocked his boots in the dirt.

Terry saw the dead actor at a walk in the yard, near the pump well, and the shotgun barrel down and rested a bent forearm, and his large round eyeglasses down at the bridge of his nose. He wore an old thick wool sweater, three buttons at the neck. He wore straight blue canvas pants and a fat brown leather belt. The pants were pulled high on his waist. He stopped front of the yard and looked serious on a dove. He put the shotgun up and sighted it, and then let the barrel drop back. He got a cigarette, no filter, put a match at his heel and struck it. He stayed on the bird awhile, and then he walked off behind the house, and he did not come back. An hour the sun went.

TWICE, IN Missouri, the car spun out from the snow, and it scared him, and he stopped at a gas station and sat in a booth and drank coffee from a white paper cup. He pondered the best way to keep the car on the road. He bought some trucker speed at the counter. He sat back down at the table and chewed one.

He started again, but the snow kept, and then it fell more, and sideways, gone on three hours.

THE TIRES bobbed again south of Cedar Rapids.

The tail pulled one way, and the hood lurched the other, and the radio was thrown at the dash, and it busted, and the cigarettes were pitched at the windshield, and then the snowbank rushed up at the hood.

He kept his hands top of the wheel. He panted in the car. He felt the blood well in his face. He shook his head, blinked hard. He squeezed the wheel, held the grip, put his forehead against the plastic between his hands.

He worried leaving was a mistake, or the way he did it was, and the snow was something like thunder, the shadow of a coming fury.

One arm jerked at the elbow and knocked on the dash. He tapped a finger against the windshield, at the snow.
  I'll go farther, he said.

He got out of the car. The snow fell soft and fast. It was quiet in the busy white.

He went to the exit. He walked the shoulder, the snow at his shins.

He came up to a gas station. The snow muddled black in the oil and the dirt, mashed to rows under tires moved slow across the lot.

He knocked his feet at the mat and went inside. He bought a can of soda, and cigarettes, and six orange crackers in plastic wrap.

He walked across the lot, to the back of a motel, and settled knees up beside a metal dumpster. He ate the orange crackers, and he drank the dark soda, and it burned his tongue, and it got dark. The air was cold, and he shifted to get warm, stood up and ran in place, pulled his arms tight to his chest. After an hour he went slow to the lobby glass, and checked the desk; there was no one. He lingered and then pushed the doors, and lowered himself slowly at a large chair backed to the front desk. He pulled his legs up on the seat.

He woke in the chair. A tiny man with a hammer stuck in his belt was shaking him on the shoulder. Terry stood and pushed the man back.

Outside the sun was out, and the snow was melting.

He walked back to the car on the interstate. The snow had puddled on the hood. He put the keys in, and the engine turned, and he laughed at the luck. The car held for a half mile, and then a belt popped, sound like a bone split, and the car lurched. He pressed the gas, and the engine revved high, and nothing, the tires a crawl.

He pulled it to the shoulder. He left the keys in the ignition and shut the door. The snow wilted. He yanked the hat down at his eyes.

H E BOUGHT a comb, a razor, a bar of soap, and a can of hairspray in the magazine store. He went to the bathroom, wet his face and his hair in the sink. He slicked his hair back with the comb. He fogged his head with hairspray. He tucked his shirt at his belt, and leaned over and pulled his socks from around his ankles. He stole a pen from the bar, and put it into his front pocket. He fished out the wedding ring.

He had seen the dead ones at the plane yard, and he saw them as dots overhead, but he never conjured being in an airplane this way, like a carnival ride or a funhouse, and he felt like he got away with something, like he owed the pilot more money.

A stewardess pushed the front curtain aside and came down the aisle. She touched the heads of the seats. Her uniform was royal blue. The stewardess put one hand on the head of the chair in front of him. She smiled and tilted her head down.

I'd like a drink, he said. A drink with alcohol.

He unlatched the tray from the back of the seat and clicked the ring on the plastic.

And a pair of wings, he said.

What kind of drink would you like? she said.

He thought for a moment. He rubbed his chin with two fingers.

A bourbon and cola, he said.

She didn't ask for identification like he expected, just smiled again and turned back down the aisle.

The plane dropped with turbulence. He kept his hands against the meal tray. The stewardess came back with the drink in one hand and a pair of wings wrapped in plastic in the other. She put them both on the tray.

Thank you, he said.

He tore the plastic open and held the wings in one hand. He couldn't push the needle down from the back of the wings. The stewardess leaned down. She smelled like soap and flowers.

Here, she said.

She pushed the pin away from the back of the wings, bunched a crease in his shirt over his heart and slid the needle through. She hooked the point back into the wings and patted his chest.

All done, she said.

He looked down at them, bronze plastic.

I like them, he said.

The stewardess went back down the aisle and pulled a curtain behind her at the end. He got one of the old dead man's pills from a pocket and swallowed it with the Coke and bourbon. He chewed ice. It was seven-thirty in the morning. He rubbed his eyes, and finished the drink, and then he put his face against the streaked glass at his right shoulder, and the propeller hummed a fast wheeze, and the wing was lit by the sun, and sky behind it, and the patched skin of the ground beneath, each one nuclear, a fission, burning and neon.

THE SNOW knotted in lit patches on both sides of a road from the airport, and the sun burned the edges. Engines whined overhead and tires wheezed on the runway. Terry quit walking, and put on the blue snow hat. He took the dope in a film can and the metal pipe from his right sock. The wind was stiff and it was hard to light. He pulled fast. The metal burned his lips. He held his breath for as long as he could, made sure it got at his blood. He stood by the side of the road and held one hand up.

79

HE GOT a ride with a slick man full of aftershave a few miles past the Denver airport. He traded some of the old man's pills for some coffee. The man kept a red thermos in the glove. He drove and poured a cup full to the plastic top and he handed it to him. They drank it steam hot, and chewed up the pills. He let him out a few miles from the dirt road, and Terry watched the car pull away, and the light slipped. He jumped around to get warm. He shook, and ground his teeth.

H E LOOKED at the back of the picture and checked the state road and the box number. He saw it matched, and then started on the road. The snow piled between the trees. In a few spots the light came through and burnt holes to the bare ground. Terry thumped the orange spike at the head of his cigarette down into the snow and put the filter in his knapsack. The light rose and fell with the slope of the road. He walked fast, got colder.

The green house was at the back of a hook in the road, through a stand of trees. There was smoke from a small chimney. He saw other houses back from the green one, red, white, green, yellow, blue.

There were small flags, the same colors as the houses, strung long in smiles across the windows. The wind put them atwitch. He jammed his eyes tight, and tried to get Alice's face in his head. He squinted to make the words written black on the flags.

He put a hand flat against the door. It was hot. The windows had pale yellow sheets draped over them. He stood there a moment, and then he knocked again, and for a long time there was nothing. He lit a cigarette and sat down next to the door.

There was a young kid with long, brown matted hair looking down at him from the doorway. He wore a beard. He rubbed his eyes and blinked a few times, and breathed out hard, didn't look him in the face. He stood back and pulled the door wide. Terry shut it behind. The latch wobbled.

The kid moved close to a shallow stone fireplace at the back of the room. There were coals in the bottom of the fire breathing orange and a split log on top. The boy sat down in a small wooden chair, poked a clothes hanger. He looked up, opened his hand a wave to the seat beside him.

Terry took off the knapsack and sat down. He did not take off the blue knit hat. He crossed his arms over his chest. He was cold. The kid poked the fire some more and it caught and wrapped the dry log. It popped, the coals jumped. The kid got up and went behind him, over to a mattress in one corner, and he sat down on the edge and jammed a glass pipe. The floor was pine, splinted and peeled, and water stained some places. There was a single mattress in all the corners, and plain wool blankets on each of them.

The kid came back over to the chair and sat down. He handed Terry the pipe. It was big as his hand, made of many colors. The kid gave him a match and motioned to the brick on the fireplace. Terry drug the match over the brick.

The smoke tasted like the red bulb on the match. It filled his chest, and he held it, and he gave the pipe back, and coughed, and couldn't stop. The kid stared at the fire and took in the smoke softly. He breathed out, and it gathered in his hair and stayed about his head and face. Terry did not stop at the cough. He lit another match and pulled, and then he coughed again, leaned over his thighs, and put forearms at his knees. He turned his head to the kid. The room was cocked toward the sun. Terry held out his hand.

The kid asked how long he needed to stay. He couldn't think straight.

I'm looking for someone, he said.

Yeah, the kid said.

He stared at the fire, struck a match and lit the bowl again. His cheeks caved and then bulged.

Where do you come from? he said.

The east, he said.

The floor cracked. Terry turned to the door. At the bottom of the window to its left, the sheet was pulled back, and left a slit. Snow fell.

The kid was named Wilson. He was from Ohio. Columbus. Other places. Athens for a little while. He had vast drawing skills. He plucked the blue hat from Terry's head and pulled it down over his squabbled hair.

The green one came first, he said. Then the red one. Then the yellow. Then the white and then the blue.

He said he was there eight months. He said he was there eleven.

She died, Terry said. Not the person I'm looking for, I mean. Her sister was my friend. Her sister is the one that's dead.

He looked back at the fire.

Everybody's got a dead sister, the kid said.

They were both quiet, and they stared at the fire a long while, and it rose, and then died, and then it flared again.

I'll take you after a little while, the kid said.

They sat quiet an hour, and then two, and Wilson stood up and went back over to the mattress in the corner. He kept the blue hat. He found another one and threw it to Terry, plain dark gray. Terry pulled the knapsack over his shoulders. Wilson put on an army jacket, sat down, and started to lace his boots.

Wilson rolled two cigarettes from a tobacco pouch before they left. The package was blue, read BUGLER on front. He pressed more pot into the bowl and lit it with a match and pulled until it smoked thick. He held the head in his right hand and opened the door.

The snow fell light, soft, and wafer thin, and the air was still. Wilson's curled fist smoked at the pipe. He pulled it again and gave it over.

Is it a long walk? Terry said.

Wilson looked confused.

No, he said.

Terry gave him the bowl. For a moment he felt like an explorer. He dreamt of maps. He stood stoned and frozen.

Wilson knocked the glass at a heel. The ash fell black and rested on top of the snow. He dropped the bowl into a pocket on the army jacket, and he put both rolled cigarettes in his mouth. He patted his chest, tapped the pockets at his hips.

Dammit, he said.

He started back toward the house.

I have a lighter, Terry said.

He kept walking, the snow dropping faster, and held up a hand.

Five minutes passed and Wilson came back with a box of matches, stood beside him and lit both cigarettes.

Lighters have bad fumes, man, he said. Toxic, I think.

Wilson passed a cigarette. Terry followed him into the woods.

They went down a hill at their backs, followed a path between fat stands of trees crowded with snow. Wilson was in front. There were footprints on the path. Terry saw one side of the green house through the trees. The yellow house was ahead. It looked the same as the green one. The trees shook, and snow fell from the branches, and then Wilson pushed the door with one hand and stood back.

You first, he said.

Terry took off his hat and put one foot onto the pine. The fire smoldered, and the air inside drifted soot.

Her back was fixed on the bend in the wall, and she sat crosslegged, on a single mattress, a wool blanket at her knees. In the other corners there were mattresses and blankets like in the green house. He went over and faced her. She knitted, he couldn't tell what, a scarf, a hat. He thought the kid meant him to talk to her.

The door shut behind him. He looked up, and then quick back to the girl. He fumbled with the hat.

Are you making a hat? he said.

She turned up, dropped her eyebrows, and pinched her mouth a smile, and then she dropped back to the cloud of red yarn and needles in her lap. He stood beside her a moment, thought about what he should say.

She stopped knitting, turned her face up, smiled. He did the same thing. He couldn't stop himself. He felt embarrassed about his bad front tooth.

Wilson coughed behind. Terry turned around. Wilson stood in the middle of the room. He pointed to a woman sat on a mattress beside the window.

She's who you want, he said.

Wilson went over to the fire and poked it with his boot. The coals caught in flame.

The woman at the window crossed her legs on the mattress, put hands flat inside of her thighs. She wore a long brown skirt draped at her knees. Her feet stuck from underneath. She wore thick gray socks.

The one with the yarn got up from the mattress and pushed past him, and then she stood next to Wilson and the fire. They both crossed their arms on their chests and the fire lit their faces orange. They leaned into each other at the hips.

Terry looked back at the woman beside the window. She was bent to her slim and white hands. She wore her hair long, like Alice, and had the same high bones at her face. He moved over and stood beside the mattress; he saw her face then, the way it moved in the light, the way it touched the light and the way the light touched it back, same as Alice, same as the picture.

He saw her sister in the field, the light hard and bright as flint.

He took off his knapsack, brought out the folded picture. He held it to her. She looked down at it, and then she turned back up to him.

It's okay, she said. Don't worry. Okay? Don't do that.

She took his right hand in her left. They looked at the picture some more.

I've hurt people, he said.

A sob caught at his face and jerked him. He didn't feel it coming. He put a hand over his eyes.

Whatever you did doesn't matter, she said.

He looked back at the fire. Wilson and the girl sat and faced it, shared a blue wool blanket over their thighs. His head leaned at her shoulder.

She let go of his hand, and then she stood up and came back with a lit joint. She held it to his lips and he pulled the smoke in. The jerk rose on him again. The room was warm. The wood in the fire whined lit ash, and it moved slow in the room, around the heads of the kid and the girl, around her sister, in the space between them. The edges burned. He felt the floor tilt. He started to fall asleep. Her sister held the joint in a fist, let it rest one knee, and she looked at him like she tried to know his name without him ever saying it out loud. She put a hand on the back of his neck and held it there.

You should sleep here, she said. You should sleep.

He nodded, and the sob caught him again. He brought his legs onto the mattress and nudged his head at her lap and shook against her.

His eyes split. He heard a flute and people moved over the floor. He was laid down, turned to the wall below the window. He coughed, put a hand at his mouth and coughed again. He wore a strange sweater. It was thick wool yarn, blue and gray and heavy over his shoulders. The wool blanket was pulled up around his stomach. He kept under the blanket, and turned over to the shadows in the room. Her sister was in the middle of the room stuck in the firelight. A man with large and wild brown hair stood beside at the fireplace. His green army pants were ripped, and his bare knees were scabbed. He arched one eyebrow to the flute in his hands. He looked possessed, or drugged, or both. Her sister came to him like a fist of smoke. She reached down and pulled him up. She pointed at the mad flute player.

He's Hungarian, she said.

She held a deep clay cup, dark and steaming, filled to the lip. She pressed it at his mouth. It burnt his tongue and throat. He drank again after she did and again after that. The flute filled the room, bodies twisted in the blue notes.

That's good, he said. Did you just make it? It tastes like squished grapes.

She shook her head, and smiled, turned back to the fire and took another sip, and they stayed like that, put their lips to the mug and moved it slow between them, and the steam wet his eyes and cheeks, and after they finished she got another cup full, and they drank that.

Terry went outside and it was cold and clear. The trees bent down and touched his head. He looked up and spoke to them.

Tap, tap, he said.

The lighter didn't work. He knocked the bottom against his palm and moved the fluid. He realized it was lit when the cigarette was half gone. He stared down at his hand, the glowing torch between his index and middle fingers, bright as a planet, lighting a pink half moon on the snow in front of him. He moved the cigarette over the snow and watched it light more of the ground pink. He laughed, leaned against the front wall of the yellow house. He heard the flute on his back. The drums began.

His eyes rolled back. He didn't know how long. The dark had a purple hue. At the rear of the house there was a stand of trees, and beneath them, toward the center, a body crouched low on a small fire.

He stood toes pointing at the yellow house and looked up into the window. He felt different, but he wasn't sure how. Her sister in the orange and black light, the other bodies, the Hungarian flute player, they all soaked to one another, and he couldn't tell the difference between any of them, he couldn't tell if they wanted to lay him down or cut off his head.

He wiped his mouth and his fingers stained purple. He thought of antifreeze. He screamed to the window, and the ones inside.

He put his hands up around his ears and hooked his fingers at the knuckles like claws.

None of it made sense, what he just did, the girl by the fire, the light in the yellow room, and the bodies twisted up. He lost some part of his head. It fell from his ears right then. He covered them with his hands. He turned around to the woods and put his back against the wall. The trees cried, the green voices of the dead coming from the needles. He slid his shoulders down the wall. He felt the splinters going in.

T HE TREES were still, and the sun out. There were footprints at the snow. Water ran from the roof onto his face. The yellow house was quiet. He sat and watched the sun move.

Her sister came out and stood beside him. She wore the same clothes. Her hair shined damp. She coughed. She looked down at him sitting there.

You're wet, she said.

I could have frozen, he said.

He wasn't sure of this.

It's too warm, she said. We knew you were okay. You were tired.

I think I could have.

He looked at his arms and legs. They felt fine. He shook them out a bit.

Look, he said. There's snow.

He swept an arm over the woods in front.

It's everywhere, he said.

The house kept you warm, she said.

He felt the back of his head, and then his shoulders, and they were warm, a little wet from dripped water.

We knew you were out here, she said. We knew.

He felt angry at the sureness of the morning, its direct whiteness, and her sister stood up in it. His head throbbed.

You're just like all of them, he said. You don't know where anyone is.

What? she said.

She looked confused.

He dropped his face to the wet snow between his legs. She blew in her hands, and they were quiet. He stood up and knocked the snow from his legs. He paced a small circle.

There's supposed to be something here, he said.

He sat down against the house once more.

There is, she said.

There's not goddammit. It's just fucking strange is all it is.

He pointed at her.

There's not anything, he said.

He shook his head.

She's supposed to be here.

She is.

Where? Tell me where.

In the trees, the snow, the mountains.

I don't believe that. I don't feel any of that.

You're not trying. You don't see.

I see plenty. I see all of it. And it's bullshit.

You are so sad.

You don't know anything.

Why can't you believe that? That she's here?

Because it doesn't mean anything.

He clenched again, and pushed at it, mashed his teeth together and cinched his eyes and he fought until it took him, and he sat in the snow and wept at his knees.

She shook her head again, breathed out hard through her nose. She went back inside the house.

Clouds beat the treeline in front, low, gray and pregnant. He stood up, stepped away from the yellow house, and pressed his shoulders to a small pine.

He found the green house. He found the road. There was the ache of snow coming on. The wind came through the trees. The prayer flags shuddered. He grew taller.

ACKNOWLEDGMENTS

Thank you people.

S. MacIntee, Terry and Brooke W, Kerry B, Barry L, Gelblums, Grace, Ian, Lisa M, D Wingo, Karey W, Ben B, Pat DG, Patrick C, J Scruggs, Katherine M, Eli, Kimi F, Christine V, Katie R, Jocelyn H, Wes P, Eric and Cindy B, C Lightsey, Wendi L, McLeods (M, C, M, J, A), M Baroody, M St. Louis, K Martin, Sara V, J McQueen, Danielle B, Erin T, Jordan L, G Singleton, Sebastian M, Scott G, Scott H, Chloe S, Munchos JC, J Marks, Joy, Megg Sully, Janelle, Kat R, Haven, Marianna S, J Ellerby, Mike W, Mark C, Phil F, Philip G, M Sanders, Gary H, J Skipper, C Howard, Hilarie B, Jeremy G, Isaac, Lauren F, Sampson, Lauren C, Jenn and JB Crane, Joanie B, Pip, Cormac, Jeff R, Rebecca A, Lee K, Amy B, Jill C, Robin H, Robyn M, Gabe H, Gabe and Mary in Maine, Susan O, Kathy P, Denis J, J Arthur, M Northridge, Julie O, Jacob, Nick M, Sabrina M, Eileen J, Maria, J Apatow, A Wise, L Misco, Clyde E, D Gessner, Nina DG, Stuart D, Nick F, Don A, Mark D, J McNally, D Bering, D Nikitas, B DeVido, A Oliver, Noah V, Benji B, Mark L, Rob B, Gary, Will, Thisbe, Kent F, J Keaney, Don R, Becky B.

Thank you schools.

Germantown Academy, Franklin & Marshall College, Western Michigan University, Northwest Missouri State, University of Iowa, Ball State University, Southern Illinois University at Edwardsville, Coastal Carolina University, Francis Marion University, University of North Carolina at Wilmington, Warren Wilson College, Sewanee, University of California at Santa Barbara, University of Alabama.

Thank you all good North Carolina Festival of the Book people.

Thank you to the many kind people I've met at bookstores, in classes, at readings, at panels and everywhere else; there are so very many of you, and your kind hearts have kept me going. My debt to you is great.

My cousins, Liz, Julie, Patrick, Eric, Carliss, Clint, Zelle, Wilson.
My aunts and uncles, Laurie, Mark and Pat, Dow and Deborah, Greg M.
My grandparents Benjamin S. and Julia Land.

Thank you parents.

Kenneth Land (who first showed me words and how one loves them and makes them).

Nancy Land (who first showed me what stong means, and what gentle means, and what care, unblinking, means).

Special thank you to the MacDowell Colony and all the good people and animals there, Michelle A, Deb, David, Blake, Mr. T, Monadnock, old Black Bear.

Special thanks to the good people at Random House, Steve Messina, Vicky Wong, Daniel Menaker, Jennifer Jones.

Thank you John Michael Johnson.
Thank you Killer Films.
Thank you David Monahan.
Thank you Sarah Messer.
Thank you David Green.
Thank you Rebecca Lee.
Thank you Wendy Brenner.
Thank you Dal Connor.
Thank you Joshua Locey.
Thank you Emile Hirsch.

Thank you John Pritchett.
Thank you Cecelia Webber.
Thank you Heather McEntire.
Thank you Selah Saterstrom.
Thank you Stephani Tewes.
Thank you John Gray.
Thank you Justin Lee.
Thank you Jynne Martin.
Thank you Kristen Foster.

I could not have made this book without the help of the following individuals.

Bill Clegg believed first and always.

Amy Williams is my sister and hero and champion and most adored.

Lee Boudreaux got everything, understood all of me, when first we spoke.

A most special thank you to Laura Ford, who granted me her steady patience and faith, and her brilliant work, and her brilliant mind; without these, I couldn't have seen this one through.

John Jeremiah Sullivan is a shaman and showed me many things I could not see but soon did.

Brett Land taught me to love the world, again, feverishly, and showed me, again, what it is a writer does.

Matthew Land taught me to work, ferociously, and without pause.

My brothers, I love you always, you are my best friends, the kindest people I know; most thanks of all be to you.

About the Author

BRAD LAND's memoir *Goat* was a national bestseller whose publishing rights were sold in six foreign countries. Land studied writing at the University of North Carolina at Wilmington and Western Michigan University. He has been a fellow at the MacDowell Colony. He lives in Carrboro, North Carolina.

About the Type

This book was set in Sabon, a typeface designed by the well-known German typographer Jan Tschichold (1902–74). Sabon's design is based upon the original letter forms of Claude Garamond and was created specifically to be used for three sources: foundry type for hand composition, Linotype, and Monotype. Tschichold named his typeface for the famous Frankfurt typefounder Jacques Sabon, who died in 1580.